"You were wearing this wedding veil when I found you," Jack told her.

She stared at the wide, satin-covered headband the gossamer fabric was anchored to which... at her jeans and athletic shoes. ...down a... ...l."

"...understand..."

"Well, that makes two of us. Maybe you were running from your wedding."

"...t?" she demanded.

"...Why would I do that..."

"...You aren't wearing an engagement ring."

"I don't know." ...nd. "I'm so confused." Her ...checked her left ha... ...ck brown lashes flutt... ...ered down, masking her fear.

Shaken, he got into the driver's seat. He would keep his distance after he got her out to the ranch. She shouldn't be around for long, anyway. Someone was bound to be missing a woman like her. Probably a man, a fiancé, maybe.

For some reason, the idea irritated Jack.

* * *

Texas Twins: Two sets of twins, torn apart by family secrets, find their way home.

Her Surprise Sister—Marta Perry
July 2012

Mirror Image Bride—Barbara McMahon
August 2012

Carbon Copy Cowboy—Arlene James
September 2012

Look-Alike Lawman—Glynna Kaye
October 2012

The Soldier's Newfound Family—Kathryn Springer
November 2012

Reunited for the Holidays—Jillian Hart
December 2012

Books by Arlene James

Love Inspired

**The Perfect Wedding*
**An Old-Fashioned Love*
**A Wife Worth Waiting For*
**With Baby in Mind*
The Heart's Voice
To Heal a Heart
Deck the Halls
A Family to Share
Butterfly Summer
A Love So Strong
When Love Comes Home
A Mommy in Mind
***His Small-Town Girl*
***Her Small-Town Hero*
***Their ... own Love*
†Anno... Small-T...
†A M... Meets H... er Mom
A M... atch Mac...
"D... other's ... Gift"
†Ba... Dreaming of a Family
†An... by Makes a ...
Th... Unlikely Match
†Se... Sheriff's Runa...
†B... cond Chance Match
... uilding a Perfect Match
... Carbon Copy Cowboy
***
***Everyday Miracles*
‡Eden, OK
†Chatam House

ARLENE JAMES

says, "Camp meetings, mission work and church attendance permeate my Oklahoma childhood memories. It was a golden time, which sustains me yet. However, only as a young widowed mother did I truly begin growing in my personal relationship with the Lord. Through adversity He has blessed me in countless ways, one of which is a second marriage so loving and romantic it still feels like courtship!"

After thirty-three years in Texas, Arlene James now resides in Bella Vista, Arkansas, with her beloved husband. Even after seventy-five novels, her need to write is greater than ever, a fact that frankly amazes her, as she's been at it since the eighth grade. She loves to hear from readers, and can be reached via her website, www.arlenejames.com.

Carbon Copy Cowboy

Arlene James

Love Inspired™

Special thanks and acknowledgment to Arlene James for her participation in the Texas Twins miniseries.

Recycling programs for this product may not exist in your area.

ISBN-13: 978-0-373-81643-9

CARBON COPY COWBOY

This edition published by arrangement with Love Inspired Books.

www.LoveInspiredBooks.com

Printed in U.S.A.

In the same way, the Spirit helps us in our weakness.
We do not know what we ought to pray for,
but the Spirit Himself intercedes for us
through wordless groans.
—*Romans* 8:26

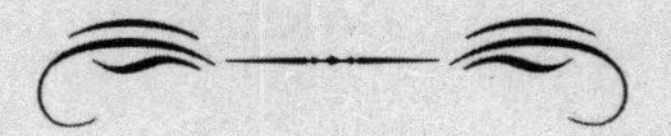

I am so blessed in my friends, especially
those upon whose prayers I can always depend.
Thank you, Joyce Powell, for the many years
of friendship and support—
and especially for the enumerable prayers.
God bless you, sweet sister.

DAR

Chapter One

"That can't be good," Jack Colby said to his grullo stallion, Tiger. Tugging his hat low over his brow, he brought the horse to a halt and leaned an elbow on the saddle horn. He judged the speed of the sleek, ruby-red coupe as he visually tracked it across the Texas landscape. "Slow it," he urged the unseen driver. "Slow it down."

Everyone in the area knew that the sharp curve at the base of Blackberry Hill was a dangerous spot. More than one driver had missed the turn and careened off the road. Some cars flipped, and one had even flown right over the bar ditch and plowed into the massive hickory tree on the other side. Nearly all of the accidents happened at night or in poor weather, but unless this particular driver slowed down, they were going to have a crash in broad daylight on a warm Monday afternoon in early September.

"Lord, help whomever's in that car," Jack prayed, "before it's too late."

Sitting tall in the saddle now, he held his breath, hoping the car would brake. Instead, it dropped out of sight, plunging down the hillside at breakneck speed.

Jack heeled the slate dun and set off at a dead gallop over the ridge, his ears tuned for the screech of brakes. He heard only a muted, metallic *thunk,* enough to tell him that the car had missed the curve. He'd been following the fence line, checking the wire for breaks, when he'd first spotted the fast-moving red car. Riding fence, the hands on the Colby Ranch called the job, as had cowboys since the first wires were strung across the open grass-lands. For Jack it was mostly a way to escape the insanity of his family life just now. Today it could be some accident victim's blessing. If he found any-one alive and got to them in time.

The grullo's powerful legs, the insides tiger-striped in shades of brownish gray, ate up the ground, flying over gullies and low bushes until Jack reined it back on its haunches. They mostly slid down the steepest part of the incline, coming to rest just before the three-strand fence. The car rested at an angle with its crumpled front fender on one side of the drainage ditch and a single rear wheel on the other. Standing in the saddle, Jack dropped the reins and vaulted over the barbed wire, hitting dirt on the opposite side with both booted feet. He then slid down the ditch and clambered over to the car. Despite its precarious position, the vehicle didn't appear to have suffered much damage. A female with long blond hair slumped over the steering wheel and through the open window trailed what looked like a long, white wedding veil.

"Hey!" Jack called. "You okay?"

The woman lay still as death, her head all but wedged into the steering wheel. Finding that he couldn't reach the driver's window from the bottom or side of the ditch, Jack quickly ran around the car. He dragged a fallen tree limb over and positioned it so that he could ease out to the passenger door, which he thankfully found unlocked.

Tossing his hat to the ground, he carefully leaned inside to reach across the empty seat and push back the lady's long hair. He intended to check her pulse, but the purity of her profile momentarily arrested his hand. In a blink, he took in the gently winged tip of her eyebrow, the delicate ridge of her nose, the prominence of her high cheekbones and the strong, clean lines of her chin and jaw. Then he saw the steady beat at the side of her slender neck and realized with great relief that she lived. A trickle of blood ran along the stitching of the leather-covered steering wheel, however, spurring Jack back into action.

Withdrawing from the car, Jack hopped down off the branch, and dug his cell phone out of his pocket. He swept his sweat-stained straw cowboy hat up off the ground and automatically plopped it down over his shaggy brown hair as he jogged toward the top of the hill. Halfway up, he picked up a decent signal and dialed the clinic in Grasslands.

"Yeah," he said to the woman who answered the phone, "this is Jack Colby. I need the doc and an ambulance out here on Franken Road. Car missed the curve at the bottom of Blackberry Hill. Female driver's alive but unconscious. Better send out a few extra fellows and some planking, too. Car's straddling the ditch. No," he said in answer to a question. "Got no idea who she is, but she's wearing a wedding veil with her jeans."

After assuring the receptionist that he wasn't kidding, Jack got off the phone and made his way back down the hill. Whoever she was, he told himself, she could thank God that she was alive. He prayed that she wouldn't wind up in a coma like his mother.

Belle Colby had fallen from a horse over two months earlier and remained unresponsive. Jack couldn't help feeling guilty because he had argued with her about their mysterious past just before she'd jumped on her grulla mare, Mouse, and charged off. Belle had always kept the past shrouded in secrecy, limiting the family to just herself, Jack and his younger sister, Violet, but he had longed to know the truth about his forebears.

He'd wanted to know if they had a father out there somewhere. Cousins? Aunts? Uncles? What about grandparents? Belle had refused to answer those questions, saying only that she was doing what was best for her children. After her accident, Jack had vowed to forget the past. But then the past had come to visit them with a vengeance, in the form of his sister Violet's identical twin, Maddie.

Jack still couldn't quite believe that he had two sisters instead of only one. Most difficult of all to accept was the fact that he, too, had an identical twin, Grayson, whom he had yet to meet. Their supposed father, Brian Wallace, who had raised Grayson and Maddie, had conveniently disappeared just after Belle's accident.

Shaking his head, Jack focused once more on the problem at hand. Clambering back down to the car, he reached in and clasped the young woman's limp hand.

"Won't be long now," he promised her. "Help's on the way."

While he waited, Jack brushed her hair from her face again, pressed his bandanna to the cut on her head until it stopped bleeding and made a cursory search of the car. Unfortunately, he came up empty and didn't find so much as a piece of paper, let alone a handbag. He noted, too, that she wore no rings, despite the wedding veil. Ten minutes later, a squad car showed up, followed by the area's lone ambulance and Doc Garth's pearly white pickup truck, which was adorned with a long, metal ladder and a couple of wide boards sticking out over the tailgate. Using the ladder to span the ditch, they laid the boards atop it, inside the rails.

After removing the bridal veil and tossing it into

the backseat of the small car, the doc—dressed in boots, jeans, a plaid shirt and pale, straw hat—did a quick examination. Outside of the clinic, the stethoscope sticking out of his shirt pocket was often the only sign of his occupation, and many of the cattlemen in the area could attest that he was as good a cowboy as he was a doctor.

"Scalp laceration," he announced. "Probably a concussion. No other obvious injuries, but she's out cold." He waved at the police officer and female nurse who served as EMTs for the Grasslands Medical Clinic. "Let's get her out of here."

While the pair worked to get the victim out of the car and onto a gurney, Jack watched from the side of the road with the fiftyish doctor and the sheriff.

"We need a warning sign up on that hill," Doc Garth decreed, pointing.

"Kids hereabouts just keep stealing it," George Cole, the Grasslands sheriff, reported laconically. A stout, balding fellow of midheight in his mid-forties, George was as laid-back as it was possible for a man in his position to be. He lifted off his tan felt hat and wiped his forehead with the sleeve of his uniform shirt, saying, "But I'll pull together some statistics and petition the county for a replacement any ol' how."

"Let me know if you need help with that," Doc said, moving aside as the gurney rolled past him. "We've had way too many accidents out here, including some fatalities." He trudged off toward the ambulance in his heavy, scuffed cowboy boots.

"I hear tell a whole family died back before my time," George commented to no one in particular. "Well," he went on, looking at Jack, "I reckon you better come into town and fill out a report, seeing as you're the closest thing we got to a witness."

"I'll do that straightaway, George," Jack promised, watching the EMTs cover the blonde's pretty face with an oxygen mask. "What do you think the deal is with that veil?" he asked.

"Don't know," the sheriff replied, gingerly crossing the ladder to poke around inside the car. "We'll ask her when she wakes up. Maybe she was running away from her wedding."

"Maybe so," Jack mused, rubbing the stubble on his chin, "but if that's true, why isn't she wearing an engagement ring or a wedding gown instead of jeans?"

"I got some more questions for you," George said, backing out of the car. "Who is this gal? She's got no ID at all unless it's in her pockets. Hey, ya'll," he called out to the medical personnel, "check her pockets for a driver's license." He waved at the vehicle, adding, "Car's got no tags, even. I noticed that right off."

Jack walked around to get a look at the back of the vehicle, which was as bare as the chief had said. "Car's a late model, though. Can't be many around."

George reached inside to turn the key in the ignition. "This baby's brand spanking new," he proclaimed. "Less than a hun'erd-fifty miles on the odometer."

"Nothing here," Doc called just then.

The sheriff parked his hands at his waist just above his gun belt and pushed out a sigh. "She's a mystery, sure enough."

Jack turned to watch as the gurney was loaded into the back of the ambulance. Lifting off his hat, he swept his hair out of his eyes. *A beautiful mystery.*

It felt as if someone had driven a spike into her head. She couldn't imagine that to be the case, but she couldn't think of anything else that could hurt like this.

A voice said, "She's coming around."

Despite having been spoken in soft, well-modulated tones, the words reverberated inside her skull like tolling bells. Moaning, she clamped her hands over her ears, aware that the movement awoke aches in other parts of her body.

"Is she all right?" asked a different voice, a masculine one that felt oddly familiar. Yet, when she tried to put a face and name together with the sound, she drew a blank.

"Back up," ordered a third voice, also masculine and quietly authoritative. She sensed a presence hovering over her, then a finger lifted her right eyelid, sending a shaft of pain straight through her eyeball. She clapped a hand over the eye, only to have the procedure repeated on the left side, blessedly with less pain. "She's conscious."

Shuffling sounds followed. Then "Miss, I have some questions for you." The words came out rough and gravelly.

"Leave her alone, George," a woman snapped.

"I got a job to do," the sheriff pointed out plaintively.

Cracking her eyelids open, she let the light bathe her retinas and sighed with the lack of pain from that quarter, at least. Emboldened, she opened up all the way and stared at the four heads bending over her. Two obviously belonged to medical personnel, the woman and a prematurely graying gentleman who was even then shrugging into a lab coat. A tag sewn to the white garment identified him as "Dr. Garth." The third face, round and balding beneath a tan cowboy hat, bore the unmistakable stamp of a cop. The last face nearly took her breath away.

So handsome that he was almost pretty, despite the dark slash of his brows peaking out from behind unkempt chestnut hair and the shadow of a beard on his smooth jawline, he had unusual dun-colored eyes—light brown like the coat of a buckskin horse, ringed with dark lashes. Everything about him screamed *Cowboy!* From the style of his faded blue shirt to the battered, sweat-stained hat that he held in his wide, long-fingered hands.

"How are you feeling?" he asked.

She watched his dusky lips forming the words, and the sound of his voice told her that she ought to know him, but she didn't. She didn't know any of them. Suddenly alarmed, she jackknifed up into a sitting position.

"Where am I?" she began, but the pain exploding inside her head stopped all but the first word. Clapping both hands over her face, she felt the bandage that covered her forehead and held back her hair. Obviously, she had been injured. Gulping back the nausea that clawed at her throat, she fixed her gaze on the doctor and rasped, "H-how many s-sutures?"

"Ten," he answered matter-of-factly.

She relaxed marginally. It couldn't be too serious, then. Ten sutures in a human seemed relatively minor, though how she knew that, she couldn't be sure. Still, she did know it. Even as she mulled that over, the pain began to recede to bearable levels. Her eardrums still throbbed, but she no longer felt as if someone had buried an ax in her skull.

"Now, then," said the voice that belonged to George, "you up to answering some questions?"

She started to nod but thought better of that and croaked, "Y-yes. You're police, aren't you?"

"That's right… George Cole, Grasslands sheriff." He stuck out a big, soft hand, which she shook carefully.

"Where is Grasslands?"

"Why, it's here, o' course," he said, glancing at

the other occupants of what was clearly an examination room.

"What am I doing here?" she asked.

"That's what we want to know," he said, dropping his hands to the gun belt that circled his thick waist. Drawing up her knees to get more comfortable, she noticed a spot of blood on her pale yellow T-shirt.

"I don't have a clue," she told him, looking up. "Can't someone tell me what's going on?"

"You wrecked your car," said the cowboy.

A car wreck. "I don't remember being in an accident."

"Jack here stayed with you until we could get the ambulance out there," the doctor clarified.

The cowboy offered his hand then, saying, "Jack Colby."

Just as she slid her hand into his, George prodded, "And your name would be…?"

She opened her mouth, but the words weren't there. "Huh," she said, frowning. "My name is…" A great void swamped her, a vast sea of absolutely nothing. "That's ridiculous," she muttered, straightening her legs again. "My name is…" She looked up, on the verge of panic, switching her gaze from one face to another until it came to rest on Jack Colby. "What is my name?" she asked, reaching out to clasp a handful of his shirt when he gave his head a short, truncated shake. "Please," she pleaded, her voice rising.

"I didn't find anything in the car with you," he

said apologetically, "no purse, no driver's license, no registration papers, nothing."

"But that doesn't make any sense!" she exclaimed. As the full import of her situation hit her, she swung her legs off the hospital bed, letting them dangle above the floor. "I don't know who I am. I don't know who I am!"

"Nurse," the doctor directed.

The patient quickly found herself lying flat on her back again while the doctor examined her and rapped out orders.

"I'm going to need a CT and a blood workup. Let's start an IV and administer a sedative."

"I don't know who I am," she repeated, trying desperately to find a way around that awful truth.

A hand fell on her shoulder. She turned her head to find the too-handsome cowboy, Jack, gazing down solemnly.

"It's okay," he told her gently. "We'll figure it out."

"I'll put out some feelers," George said. "Even without a license plate on the car, we ought to get something off the VIN."

"What? No license plates?" she asked. "How is that even possible?"

"That's what we was hoping you could tell us," the sheriff pointed out, adding, "you're gonna need to stick around until we figure this thing out. I'll see if there's any stolen car reports or missing persons in the area that fit."

"Stolen!" she gasped. "B-but I would never... That is, I can't imagine..." Yet, how could she know what she'd do when she didn't even know her own name?

"It's just a formality," Jack Colby assured her, looking pointedly at George, who waved a hand.

"SOP. Standard Operating Procedure. Now, why didn't I think to bring along a camera? Doc, you got any way to take her photo so I can circulate it around?"

"Here, I'll do it," Jack said, pulling out his phone. While he snapped the photo, George grumbled about the city refusing to buy him and his deputies the latest smartphones. "What's your email address?" Jack interrupted, saving the picture to his phone. George told him, and the cowboy sent the photo off with a swooshing sound.

"That'll sure make things easier," George told him. "Won't even have to scan it up before sending it out."

The subject of the photograph didn't know whether to hope someone recognized her or not, considering that her likeness would be going out to law-enforcement agencies.

As if he sensed her dilemma, George smiled and patted her hand. Then he ruined the gesture by saying, "Just don't leave the county, little lady, until I tell you it's okay."

Her eyes widened as a whole new problem

emerged. “Where am I going to stay? Do I even have any money?”

“Didn’t find any,” Jack murmured sympathetically.

“You’ll be staying right here for the time being,” the doctor decreed. “I want you here for observation at least for tonight.”

“That’s good enough for now,” George decided. Turning to leave, he doffed his hat, saying, “I’ll be in touch.”

Her mind whirling, she closed her eyes. “Lord, help me,” she whispered fervently. “Lord, help me.”

She felt a warm, gentle touch at her throat and looked up to find Jack Colby fingering a small gold cross at the end of a delicate gold chain looped about her neck. Looking at that cross gave her a small sense of peace; yet she couldn’t recall ever having seen it before this moment.

“Well, you’re a believer,” Jack said, smiling crookedly. “That’s a help.”

She gave him a tremulous smile. “Yes, that’s a help.”

He dropped the cross. “I’ll say a prayer for you, then.”

“Thank you,” she replied. “Uh, f-for everything.”

“Aw, I didn’t do anything special,” he said, moving toward the open doorway. Pausing, he swept back his hair with one hand and plunked his hat down over it with the other. “I wouldn’t worry too much if I was you,” he said kindly.

"Your memory's apt to return on its own at any time," the doctor added helpfully.

"But what if it doesn't?" she had to ask.

"George will figure it out," Jack reassured her, "or somebody will come looking for you."

She gulped, wishing that made her feel something less than terrified.

Well, that was that. Jack stepped out onto the graveled parking lot of the medical center. Car wrecks and amnesiac blondes made for an exciting first Monday of the month. He hoped this wasn't a sign of how the rest of September would go, though. July and August had been dramatic enough, what with his mother's accident, his sister Violet meeting her previously unknown twin Maddie, his own still-unknown twin Grayson off on an undercover assignment, their supposed father disappearing, a half brother he'd never met overseas with the military… Jack had more questions now than he'd had the day of his mother's accident.

If all that weren't enough, Violet had become engaged to Maddie's former fiancé, and now Maddie was going to marry the Colby Ranch foreman, Ty. Jack couldn't imagine why anybody in his right mind would get entangled in a romance under such circumstances—or any other, when it came right down to it. That way, as he well knew, lay heartache.

Automatically, his thoughts went to his former girlfriend Tammy Simmons, but then another face flashed before his mind's eye. Taking out his phone, he tapped the photo icon. Her image instantly came up. She looked small and frightened with that bandage on her forehead and her big, deeply set hazel eyes begging him to tell her who she was. He didn't think he'd ever forget how horrified she'd looked when she'd realized that she couldn't recall her own name.

He knew a little of what she was feeling. He and his sisters had gone to Fort Worth in search of answers about their past. They all needed to understand why their parents had split up the family and kept it a secret from them. According to an old neighbor, Patty Earl, her late husband, Joe, was his and Grayson's real father. It didn't make sense for Brian to raise Grayson in that scenario, but Brian's disappearance felt awfully convenient to Jack. A doctor, Brian had supposedly gone to South Texas on a medical mission trip and had somehow fallen off the face of the earth—just when there were questions to be answered.

If only his mother would wake from her coma and give them those answers. Jack doubted that he could accept them from anyone else, not even Brian Wallace. Now Jack had more questions than ever, and he had to wonder if he even knew who he was. Obviously, his last name wasn't Colby, but it might not be Wallace, either. Jack found the whole situation maddening.

But maybe not as maddening as amnesia. Jack

gazed down at the blonde whose photo he'd taken with his phone.

His heart went out to her. Even if she turned out to be a car thief or an escaped mental case, not knowing the truth had to be awful. And there again, he could relate.

He dropped the phone back into his pocket and walked out to the truck that he'd driven in from the ranch. After the accident, he'd ridden Tiger back to the barn at the main compound then come straight here to the Grasslands Medical Clinic.

Everyone around town referred to the clinic as a hospital, but in truth, it was nothing more than a converted house with a pair of examining rooms, a small lab, a couple of offices and four or five beds in a dormitory-type setting. Serious cases got transferred to Amarillo with long-term ones going to the skilled nursing center here in Grasslands, otherwise known as Ranchland Convalescent Home. It was more or less an old-folks' home, a place where his vibrant, forty-three-year-old mother did not belong, but he was glad to have her closer to home now.

At least he and his sisters could function somewhat normally, and one or the other of them visited Belle almost daily. Jack stopped in there as soon as he left the clinic, anxious to tell her about his unusual day.

He could only hope that she would hear him.

Chapter Two

They had seen to it that Belle had a private room with all the monitoring equipment and nursing care that she needed, but if she even knew those things, no one could tell. Jack spoke to her as if she could hear him, telling her about the day's adventure. She appeared to sleep peacefully through his monologue, her long auburn hair spread out on the pillow beneath her head, the gentle rise and fall of her chest the only sign that she lived. As always, Jack sat beside her bed and prayed.

Oh, Lord, please let her wake up and be well. Please. And the blonde lady, too. She obviously needs a helping hand right now.

He added pleas for clarity on the issues troubling the family before rising to kiss his mother's smooth forehead.

"I'm sorry, Mama," he whispered, for perhaps the thousandth time. "Please come back to us. We need you more than ever."

Feeling low, he trudged out to his dirty, white pickup truck and slid behind the steering wheel. Then he started the engine and drove out to the ranch. As he turned the truck through the massive gate with its rock columns and metal arch displaying the Colby Ranch brand, Jack thought again of the lovely blonde back there in the hospital.

No doubt, she worried about where she would stay and how she would live until her memory returned. Without money, she really had no options. Grasslands didn't have a homeless shelter because it didn't have any homeless. She couldn't stay at the clinic for long, either, but someone would surely take her in—someone with plenty of room.

Sighing as the imposing ranch house came into view, Jack mentally cataloged the house that he, his mom and two sisters occupied. There was room for her. That didn't mean that he had to offer a bedroom to the pretty amnesiac, though, even if he had been the one to rescue her from a car wreck.

Of course, it didn't mean that he shouldn't, either.

He supposed they could open one of the old, unoccupied cabins on the place, but it didn't seem wise for a woman with a head wound serious enough to cause amnesia to stay alone. Too bad the hotel in town was closed temporarily because the couple who owned and operated it had been called away on a mission of mercy to help family members who had been burned out by wildfires in the central part of the states. Jack went so far as to consider calling the pastor at the Grasslands Community Church to see if he could find a host for the woman, but in the normal course of things when temporary shelter was needed, the first phone call that the good reverend would make would be to the Colbys.

"Aw, come on, Lord," Jack grumbled aloud. "Don't we have enough trouble as it is?"

Unfortunately, the Lord, as was His habit, didn't say a word. Jack heard Him, nevertheless.

Jack turned the truck through the gate in the wrought-iron fence that separated the main house from the rest of the compound, parked and climbed out, trudging into the house through the carport door. He'd barely set foot in the back hall before Lupita, the housekeeper and cook, stuck her head out of the kitchen.

"Dinner in five minutes."

"Already?" he asked, hanging his hat on a peg fixed to the wall. He pulled his phone from his pocket to check the time. Man, this day had flown. "I'll wash up," he muttered, heading for his room.

For some reason, he swiped his thumb across the bottom of the screen on his phone and watched as the blonde's photo popped up again. He stopped in the dining room, aware that his sisters—he still couldn't get over the fact that there were two of them and how alike they looked now that Maddie had taken to jeans and boots—busily laid the table for the evening meal.

"Oh, good, you're home," Violet said, smiling as she placed a napkin beside a plate.

"Uh-huh." Disturbed by his compulsion to stare at the picture on his phone, he tossed the small device down at his regular place. "Y'all ought to know that we could be having company soon."

"Oh?" Maddie said, closing a drawer in the breakfront. "Who? Have you heard from Grayson?"

Jack made a face at the mention of his brother. "No, I haven't heard from Grayson, and I don't expect to. Why would I?"

"He *is* your twin," Violet pointed out.

"So? I'm not talking about him. This is someone different.... A person was in a car wreck today."

"Oh, wow!" Violet exclaimed. "Anyone we know?"

"Some woman who didn't make the curve at the bottom of Blackberry Hill," Jack answered carelessly. "She's going to need a place to stay when Doc says she can leave the hospital."

"When will that be?" Maddie asked.

He shrugged. "Soon, I expect."

"Will she need nursing?" Violet queried apprehensively.

"No, nothing like that," he assured them, more gruffly than he'd intended. "I'll explain later. If it comes to it, I mean. She might stay somewhere else. Now, I better wash up."

He walked off toward the back staircase. The very moment that he rounded the corner, he heard Violet say, "I might have known."

Drawing to a halt at the note of concern in her voice, he retraced his steps to the doorway and saw that she'd picked up his phone and unlocked the screen. She and Maddie stood huddled together beside the dining table, as alike as two peas in a pod, staring down at the photo of the blonde woman now at the clinic.

"She's probably tall and leggy," Violet muttered, putting down the phone.

As a matter of fact, she is.

"What makes you say that?" Maddie asked, and Jack mentally echoed the question. *Yeah, what makes you say that?*

"Because," Violet answered, "that's the type Jack goes for."

Jack darted up his forehead as Maddie surmised, "You're describing the girl that broke his heart last year, aren't you?"

Violet nodded. "Long legs, long blond hair, blue eyes."

Hazel, Jack corrected silently, then he remembered that Violet was describing Tammy, not his car-wreck victim in the wedding veil.

"What happened there, anyway?" Maddie asked.

Jack leaned a shoulder against the door frame and prepared to listen to Violet's thoughts on the subject, intrigued primarily because they'd never discussed the issue.

"Jack and Tammy dated all throughout high school," Violet reported. "Then when Jack went off to college, she broke up with him."

Not exactly. It had been a mutual decision at that point. Jack had wanted the freedom to enjoy his college experience, and Tammy hadn't wanted to sit home waiting for him to graduate. It had seemed sensible at the time to give each other some freedom. They'd dated off and on over the next four years, then Tammy had gotten involved with someone else. They had broken up when he was transferred. Jack had assumed that she'd objected to moving away from Grasslands, but it had turned out that she'd been unwilling to trade one "nothing town" for another, as she'd put it.

"For a long time, everyone thought Tammy would marry the manager at the ranch supply store," Violet went on, "but after he left town, she and Jack started dating again. When Jack started fixing up the old Lindley house, everyone thought for sure that they would get married."

From the moment he'd seen that place as a teenager, Jack had thought he'd like to live there when he grew up and got married, and he'd said as much when his mother had bought the acreage after old man Lindley had died. He hadn't realized how seriously his family had taken his plans to heart until now.

"That's the one he's been working on since I came here, isn't it?" Maddie asked sadly, and Violet nodded.

Jack had taken refuge at the old house off Franken Road. Gutting the kitchen, replacing floorboards and squaring up the doorways had taken his mind off the turmoil that Maddie's arrival in their lives had engendered, but he hadn't meant to make her feel bad by disappearing. It was just his way. He wasn't used to having two sisters, let alone his mom in a coma and all these questions about a family he hadn't even known he had. Staying to himself and working hard kept his mind off those problems. He'd rebuilt the staircase after Tammy had left town, but that's where he'd left it until his mother's accident. Once it had become obvious that Belle would remain in a coma, Jack had torn out and replaced the bath fixtures at the old house.

"Yes, Jack's always intended to live there," Violet went on, "but apparently Tammy didn't get that. Her parents, Gabe and Gwen Simmons, down at the coffee shop, say that Tammy had been telling them that she was getting out of Grasslands, either with Jack or someone else. Apparently, when Jack asked her to marry him, she told him that she'd marry him only if he took her away from Grasslands. He wasn't about to leave here, so they broke up." She sighed. "Not long after, she left town with a trucker who was passing through. We've heard that she's in Houston now."

It wasn't quite that simple, Jack mused. He'd been fixing up the house as a surprise for Tammy. He'd bought a diamond ring and staged his proposal in front of the newly rebuilt rock fireplace in the front room, but when Tammy had realized that he'd meant for them to live there, she'd laughed at him.

"I'm not going to stay around here any longer than I have to," she'd said. *"Just tell your mother that you want your inheritance now, and let's go someplace fun."*

Shocked, he'd informed her that he would never leave the ranch, at which point Tammy had declared that he could keep his ring. She'd been seeing the trucker all along, it seemed, and the guy had promised to take her somewhere exciting, someplace where "cowboys and cows were not the be all and end all." She'd left him that day saying that she'd wasted enough time on him.

"No wonder Jack wants no part of love," Maddie observed.

"I don't know," Violet said, staring down at his phone. "Maybe he's ready to move on, after all."

A picture of the girl in the hospital bed suddenly shimmered through Jack's mind. He saw her beautiful eyes open, her gaze flicking around the room and coming to rest on him. She had smiled slightly, as if she'd recognized him. He'd had to restrain himself from stepping forward to touch her. Every protective instinct he possessed had risen to the fore, and he couldn't have stopped himself from trying to reassure her.

He recalled the moment when she'd realized that she'd lost her memory. The panic and horror in her eyes had pierced him. He'd wanted to wrap her in his arms and promise her that all would be well. He'd never felt that way toward Tammy or any other woman outside of his mom and Violet.

Chills ran down Jack's spine. He shifted away from the door frame and stepped back. What was he thinking? What was Violet thinking? Just because he felt a little protective toward an injured woman and had taken a picture of her for the local police, that didn't mean he was interested in her *personally.* No way. Even if the woman hadn't been in dire straits, the timing couldn't have been worse. With his mom in a coma and all this upheaval in the family, romance was simply out of the question.

"We don't know anything about this woman," he heard Maddie caution. Jack snorted. No one knew anything about this woman. She didn't even know anything about herself! "We need to pray about this," Maddie added.

Sounded like good advice to Jack, very good advice. He'd pray for the mysterious young woman in the wedding veil and blue jeans and ask the Lord to meet her needs before the Colbys had to step in. That would be one problem solved, at least. The rest would resolve in time. Or not. He truly wasn't sure that he even cared anymore.

Did it really matter why Belle and Brian had split up the family, including two sets of twins? His mother had been determined to keep the secret, and he should have let her. He shouldn't have insisted that she tell him why they had no contact with any extended family. If he'd let it alone then, his mom might not be lying in that hospital bed now. As far as he was concerned, the whole matter should just be dropped.

Turning, he went to clean up before Lupita could catch him eavesdropping.

Sitting on the edge of the hospital bed, she curled one leg beneath her and smiled at the fashion dolls "walking" across the coverlet in the hands of little Emily Wilmon, the only other patient in the dormitory.

"I think you look like a Julia," the child said, as if amnesia was some sort of game.

"Julia?" She laughed, shaking her blond head. "Why do you think that's my name?"

Emily looked at the male doll in her left hand and changed her mind. "Kenna!" she decided. "I want your name to be Kenna!"

Struck by how right that sounded, she sucked in a deep breath, murmuring, "Kendra, maybe?"

"Yeah, Kendra." Emily beamed.

"Who is Kendra?"

The husky, masculine voice shivered through her with welcome familiarity. She looked up to find Jack Colby standing in the break between the curtains surrounding her bed. Hatless, his rich brown hair fell forward haphazardly, giving him a sweetly boyish air. Much as the day before, he wore scuffed brown boots, comfortable jeans, a utilitarian belt with a palm-size buckle engraved with the initials J. C. and a long-sleeved shirt. He held that disreputable, sweat-stained straw hat in his hands. Only the shirt seemed to have changed. The faded but sunny gold of this one made his light brown eyes glow.

"I guess Kendra is me for the time being," she told him, winking at Emily. "Seems as good a name as any."

"So still no memories?" he asked casually, stepping closer.

"Obviously I remember how to speak and how to walk and how to brush my hair, but I can't recall a thing about me personally." She shook her head. "It's as if yesterday was the first day of my life."

Nurse Hamm had graciously laundered her clothing the previous night, so she had been happy to change out of the hospital gown and into her own things that morning. The dark jeans, pale yellow T-shirt and white athletic shoes felt familiar and safe, but she couldn't recall purchasing them. Were they favorite items or merely garments to wear? She just did not know.

"Met George outside," Jack stated offhandedly.

George Cole had been by earlier to tell her that he hadn't found any reports of a missing person or vehicle that matched the descriptions he'd put out county-wide, so he was broadening the scope of his search. Meanwhile, she was not to leave the area. As if she could do so on foot without a penny to her name.

"He's, um, running the Vehicle Identification Number on the car and contacting police departments within the odometer range."

Jack nodded. "So he said. Since no one within the mileage on the odometer of the car seems to know you, he's searching the state database for the VIN."

"What if it's not there?"

"I don't know," Jack said. "I guess the car would have to be from out of state. Could've been brought in by a new-car dealer."

"A new-car dealer," she murmured, feeling uneasy.

"What?" Jack asked.

She searched her mind for some reason to explain her feeling but found nothing, so she shook her head. "I don't even remember the car, let alone where I got it."

The curtain slid back, and Dr. Garth entered the space. "Emily," he said, taking the child by the shoulders and bodily turning her, "you're supposed to be in bed. Nurse Hamm has medicine for you, and your mom's off work now. She'll be here any minute. Scoot."

Uncowed, Emily tucked her dolls into the curve of one arm and waved. "Bye, Kendra!"

"Bye, sweetie."

"Kendra?" Dr. Garth asked, sliding his hands into the pockets of his white lab coat.

"Emily named me after her boy doll."

"Ah. The amnesia hasn't alleviated, then?"

She shook her head, sighing. "No."

Jack Colby chuckled, watching Emily scamper across the room to her own bed. "Could've been worse," he noted drily. "I can think of a few toys and cartoon characters I wouldn't want to be named after."

"Kendra" shared a wan smile with him. It was true that she preferred that moniker to a number of other possibilities, but what she wouldn't give to merely know her own name. Choking back a fresh threat of panic, she squared her shoulders and faced the doctor.

"Am I ever going to remember?" she asked.

He pulled in a deep breath before carefully saying, "It's impossible to know. Amnesia has no rules. Your memory may never return. On the other hand, you could wake up one morning with everything in place, or something could trigger full recall. Or your memories could come back bit by bit."

"Kendra feels familiar somehow," she reported, excited to think that might mean something significant.

"But it doesn't trigger anything definite?" he asked.

Deflated, she dropped her gaze. "No. Nothing."

"Worrying about it won't help," he told her kindly.

"What does?" she asked, feeling glum again.

"Time. Hopefully."

She spread her hands. "Seems I have plenty of that."

"Do you have any idea where you're going to spend that time?" the doctor asked. "There's really no reason to keep you here any longer, and we have so few beds…."

Alarm rose in her chest again. "I—I'd hoped you might have a suggestion."

"Actually," Jack said, shifting his weight from foot to foot, "I do. My sisters and I would like to invite you to stay out at the ranch."

"There you go!" Doc said with obvious relief. "Problem solved."

On one hand, she wanted to throw her arms around Jack Colby and sob with gratitude, but what did she know of this man, really? Of anyone here? Even herself.

"I—I wouldn't want to impose on anyone."

"You won't be imposing," Jack insisted. "The house is plenty big, and there's a room in the same wing with my sister, Maddie. You won't be in anyone's way."

"But… You don't know me." *And I don't know you,* she thought.

"The Colby Ranch is a good place for you," Doc said. "The Colbys are good Christian folk, and Violet and Maddie are about your age. Now, I'll want you back in about ten days to have those stitches removed," he proclaimed, as if that settled the matter, and she guessed it did. What other option did she have, after all?

"Thank you," she said to Jack, but he just looked away with a slight shrug.

Dr. Garth stepped forward to pull a pair of gloves from a container fixed to the wall above her bed. "I'll just take a gander at this before you go." After donning the gloves, he peeled away the bandage. "Looks fine. Wait another forty-eight hours before you shampoo your hair. Then just keep dirt out of the incision." He applied a large adhesive dressing and peeled off the gloves. "Normally, we'd have you sign some papers and arrange payment before you go, but in this case, we'll wait a bit. We'll take care of it when you've figured things out."

"Sounds good," she said, greatly relieved. "Thank you."

The doctor nodded, first at her, then at Jack. "Wait here. I'll send Nurse Hamm over with a few things—a kind of parting gift we give our patients. Toiletries, mostly."

"Thanks again," she murmured.

"See you soon," the doctor told her, adding pointedly, *"Kendra."*

She smiled because of his kindness but also because she found it surprisingly easy to think of herself as Kendra. Now, if she only knew what kind of a person "Kendra" was.

I ought to let Doc examine my *head while I'm here.* Jack was walking beside "Kendra" across the clinic parking lot. His mood pretty much matched the overcast day. He couldn't help feeling somewhat responsible for her, and with the only hotel in the area temporarily closed, he had no choice but to take her home with him until George said she could leave. That didn't mean he was happy about it, though. He would have felt better about the underling if he hadn't had her on his mind the entire day long. For once, he couldn't seem to focus his thoughts where he focused his energies, and that bothered him. He told himself that it was because of the unusual circumstances. Amnesia! How often did that happen? At least she wasn't in a coma.

Turning off thoughts of his mother, whom he'd visited before walking over to the clinic, he opened the passenger door of the truck for Kendra—he really had no other way to think of her—and handed her up inside, making sure that she didn't bump her head along the way. Tucking the small plastic bag of bottles and tubes into the floorboard, she murmured her thanks and reached for her safety belt.

"You okay with this?" he asked. When she gave him a blank look, he turned toward her. "I had a buddy who crashed his car back in college," Jack explained. "It was weeks before he could bear to ride in the front seat of a vehicle again."

"I don't remember the crash, so it doesn't bother me," she said with a shrug.

"Right. Well, that's one good thing about amnesia, I guess."

She frowned, looking so sad that he wanted to bite his tongue.

He searched his mind for something helpful to say and came up with "My sisters can lend you some things to wear. But, um, not jeans, I imagine. You're pretty tall."

"Am I?" she asked, looking down at herself.

Man, if she was faking amnesia, she was doing a good job of it. Jack couldn't quite believe that to be the case, however.

"You're for sure taller than my sisters," he told her, his gaze sweeping down the length of her legs. Long, slender legs. "I'd say five-eight, maybe five-nine."

"I see."

"We can stop by the ranch supply store and pick up some things, if you like."

She shook her head, long blond hair cascading against her shoulders. "I'd rather wait until I can pay."

"Whatever you say," he told her doubtfully.

"Let's wait another day or two, anyway," she decided. "In case the police come up with something."

He told himself not to be too pleased that she

hadn't jumped at his offer to buy her some new clothes. Still, that made her more believable.

Her slender brows drew together. "Did anyone look in the trunk of my car for a suitcase?"

"Not while I was there," Jack answered. "You feel up to going to take a look now?"

"Oh, yes. Please," she said eagerly.

"Car's over behind the gas station," he said, closing her door. He hurried around the truck and got in behind the steering wheel, thinking that maybe seeing the car would jar loose her memory of herself. Maybe the Lord was just waiting for her to see that sleek red car before He opened the door to her past.

And maybe, just maybe, God had something else in mind entirely.

Chapter Three

"Grasslands is such a small town that we don't have a real police impound," Jack explained.

"Grasslands," she echoed thoughtfully.

"Does that sound familiar?" he asked, starting up the engine.

"I don't know," she said as he backed the truck around, "but I keep wondering why I was headed here."

"Are you sure you were?"

She heaved a great sigh. "I just don't know, but George said that the road I was on doesn't go anywhere else."

"Well, it's true that Franken Road dead-ends right here in town, but there are other roads leaving town, you know."

"So maybe I was just passing through," she muttered.

"Could be."

They discussed where she might have been going,

if not Grasslands, but none of it really made any sense. If she had been headed for Lubbock or any point in between, there were much more direct routes. Same for Childress and Wichita Falls. She'd been traveling in the wrong direction for her destination to have been Amarillo, Dimmitt or Muleshoe.

When they got to the gas station, which was also a convenience store and mechanic's shop, Jack pulled around back. As he suspected, the car had been left unlocked. He found the remote trunk latch inside and popped it.

"Nothing," Kendra announced, sounding deeply disappointed.

Jack reached into the backseat and grabbed the veil to show her. "There's this."

"This was in the car?" she asked with a frown as she reluctantly took the long, sheer piece of lace-edged fabric into her hand.

"You were wearing it when I found you."

Her jaw dropped as the gossamer material filtered out of her hand and wafted on the breeze. "*Wearing* it?" She stared at the wide, satin-covered headband to which the fabric was anchored, then looked down at her jeans and athletic shoes. "I don't understand."

"Well, that makes two of us. Maybe you were running from your wedding."

"Why would I do that?" she demanded.

Jack shook his head. "Don't know. You aren't wearing an engagement ring."

She checked her left hand, verifying the truth of his statement. “I’m so confused.”

“You don’t recognize the car, even?”

Walking slowly around the driver’s side of the bright red coupe, she shook her head, but when she came to the front, she stopped and stared at the crumpled bumper.

“Was I in the backseat?” she asked after a moment.

“No. You were driving.”

Her eyes grew wide. “No! I—I remember being in the backseat! And there were other people in the car.”

“Not this car,” Jack stated firmly. “You were alone, behind the wheel and wearing that veil when I got to you.” He pointed to the fabric now crumpled in her arms.

“Maybe they ran away before you got there,” she proposed.

“No way. I arrived right after the crash. Besides, the car was suspended over a ditch. No one could have gotten out of this car without help. Doc had to make a bridge from a ladder and planks to get to you.”

She gulped. “But I had this flash of… I could see the backs of their heads, and the car was sliding so fast.”

“Could be you imagined it,” he surmised, “or maybe it’s a memory of another accident. Think back. Who are these people you remember?”

Frowning, she seemed to turn her gaze inward. After a moment, she shook her head. "I don't know. It was just a flash. Two people in the front seat and me in the back." Her face screwed up with the effort to remember. "There's nothing else. Nothing."

She looked so helpless that he had to quell the urge to slip a comforting arm around her. Instead, he said, "We ought to get on our way. Lupita will have supper ready soon."

"Lupita?" she asked in a dull voice.

"Our housekeeper and cook."

"Hmm."

She barely seemed to notice that he turned her toward his truck and opened the truck door for her. He had to take her by the arm and all but lift her up into the seat.

"You've been very kind," she said suddenly, fixing those hazel eyes on him.

He felt like he was staring straight into her frightened soul. Then her thick brown lashes fluttered down, masking her fear.

Shaken, he once again moved around the truck and got into the driver's seat. He told himself as they drove through town that he would keep his distance after he got her out to the ranch. His sisters and Lupita could take care of her, make her feel welcome. She shouldn't be around for long, anyway. Someone was bound to be missing a woman like her. Probably a man, a fiancé, maybe.

For some reason, the idea irritated Jack. But, then, he reasoned, everything irritated him lately.

Watching the storefronts pass by on the tree-lined main street, Kendra felt an odd sense of familiarity. Yet, she could not recall ever having seen any of the businesses before this moment, not the Grassland Coffee Shop or the Ranch House Bakery or the Corner Drug Store, not the Grasslands Bank or the library or the school. She stared at the Grasslands Community Church as Jack brought the truck to a brief halt at the four-way stop sign on the edge of the small-town green.

The sanctuary was a modest building of all white, from the tip of its tall steeple to the painted concrete steps leading to the white-paneled door tucked beneath a peaked overhang. She stared, transfixed, at the stately chapel, which sat in simple splendor among the pecan trees and graveled walkways on the green lawn. Behind it stood a more modern building, and between the two lay graveled paths winding through a garden of shrubs, rosebushes and flowerbeds. A prayer garden, she surmised, judging by the white cross that rose between a pair of crepe myrtles. Kendra felt a sudden, wrenching need to kneel there and beg God to return her memories to her, but Jack had already started the truck on its way again.

Had this, then, been her destination? But if she had been on her way to Grasslands when she'd wrecked the car, why didn't someone here recognize her?

She looked down at the veil in her hands and shivered. Had she been running from someone or something? But who or what?

Did someone out there miss her, need her, want her? Or was she as alone in this world as she felt? Alone, except for the cowboy behind the steering wheel. Suddenly, Jack Colby had become her lifeline in a cold and tumultuous sea of confusion.

"Your ranch is farther from town than I thought," Kendra remarked.

Jack cocked a shoulder in a truncated shrug. "It's a big ranch."

"I see."

A big ranch apparently required a big gate, for they soon came upon one. Slowing the truck, Jack turned it between the square, head-high rock columns and guided it over the cattle guard beneath the metal arch with a circle at its apex. Inside the circle, three Cs intertwined.

"Is that your brand?" she asked, referring to the letters inside the circle above their heads.

"Yep. The three Cs are for my mom, me and my sister, Violet."

"I thought I heard you say 'sisters,' plural."

"Uh-huh. The other is Maddie."

"But she's not part of the ranch?"

Jack shifted in his seat. "Well, she lives here," he said vaguely.

Kendra wanted to ask why the brand didn't have four Cs then, but she decided to keep her comments to herself as the truck accelerated along the straight, graveled drive, barbed wire flanking it on both sides.

A number of structures came into view. First, a corral built of metal pipe on the left. Straight ahead stood a magnificent two-story house constructed of native stone and brown brick. All graceful arches and mullioned windows with a porch across the front, it sat surrounded by mature trees and a wrought-iron fence. Behind it stood a number of cottages, some in better shape than others, several sheds and a large metal barn sprouting corrals and pens on both sides. Sand-colored with a green roof, the barn drew Kendra's eye. She felt an odd yearning and wondered what animals resided within.

"I see that you keep horses in the barn," she ventured eagerly.

Jack nodded. "Personal stock, mostly."

"Cows, too, I imagine."

He gave her an odd look. "Two at the moment, an ailing calf and a late springer."

A late springer. "A heifer giving birth later than normal," she muttered, wondering how she knew that.

"You've been on a ranch before?" Jack asked,

turning the truck through a second gate, a smaller version of the first one.

"It would seem so," she told him. "I don't remember it, though. Do you have any other animals around?"

"Sure," Jack said. Ignoring the sweeping gravel drive in front of the house, Jack guided the truck around to the side of the building. "Pigs, chickens, goats. We try to be as self-sufficient as possible."

She nodded, thinking about that. "Are you using the goats for cheese and milk or butchering?"

"Cheese and milk." He brought the truck to a halt beneath a large covered parking area that sheltered a trio of other vehicles. "You've been around animals." A statement, not a question.

"It would seem so," she agreed.

"Well, you're in the right place, then," he told her, nodding at a dog that trotted into view. "That's Nipper."

"Brindle Australian shepherd," she said, amazed that she knew these things.

A young woman with long auburn hair caught in a ponytail at the nape of her neck followed the dog into the carport, slapping a pair of leather gloves against one jeaned thigh.

"That's my sister, Violet," Jack said, opening his door.

Feeling suddenly shy, Kendra slowly slid from the truck to the concrete floor of the carport.

"Hey, y'all," Violet greeted them as Nipper trotted

over to give Jack a doggy grin. He bent to ruffle the dog's fur.

"Sis, this is our new guest."

"Call me Kendra," she said, putting out her hand.

Violet gripped her hand with her own smaller one. "Hello, Kendra. Nice to meet you. Welcome to the Colby Ranch."

"Thank you. I'm very grateful for the invitation."

"I understand that you were in an accident."

Kendra glanced at Jack. "Yes."

"She doesn't remember anything about it," Jack said, avoiding Kendra's gaze.

Violet lifted her slender brows. "That might be for the best. I hear a lot of folks don't remember accidents. Things just happen too fast to register sometimes, I guess."

"Actually," Kendra said hesitantly, looking to Jack again, "I don't remember anything at all." Realizing that he hadn't told his sister about the amnesia, she quickly added, "About myself, I mean. I—I don't even remember my own name. I don't know where I'm from, why I was on that road.... Nothing."

Violet stood with her mouth open for several heartbeats, then she suddenly lurched forward and wrapped her arms around Kendra. "You poor thing!"

Kendra blew out a breath, relieved beyond words. "Thank you. I don't know what I'd have done if your family hadn't invited me to stay here."

Violet abruptly backed up, turning her chocolate-brown eyes on her brother. “Yeah. Huh.” She smiled at Kendra. “No problem. Come on in. Dinner will be ready soon.”

Jack lifted a hand to indicate the door, still not meeting Kendra’s gaze. She followed Violet through a hallway tiled with large white squares and on through an open doorway into a kitchen the size of a small airplane hangar. Outfitted with rich, dark woods, pale granite and stainless steel, it boasted a work island easily twelve feet long. Various pots bubbled and simmered on a six-burner, professional-quality stove, watched over by a small, brown-skinned woman, presumably the aforementioned Lupita, with long, dark, silver-streaked hair.

One end of the room opened to an octagonal breakfast area with a large, square table at its center. A carbon copy of Violet with shorter hair stood over a young girl seated at the table, schoolbooks spread out before her.

“Maddie and Darcy, this is Kendra,” Violet said.

“Twins,” Kendra blurted as the woman looked up at her.

The girl, who appeared to be about eight, had a brown ponytail and brown eyes. She smiled at Jack, who winked at her.

Maddie laughed. “Yes.” She nodded at Jack, saying, “He’s a twin, too, you know. He and our brother Grayson.”

Kendra looked at Jack, who frowned before muttering, "I'm gonna get washed up."

"Dinner in fifteen minutes!" the Hispanic woman at the stove called.

Jack nodded and walked out of the room. Kendra watched him go with a sinking heart. Feeling lost and alone, she smiled awkwardly at the two young women watching her with curious, identical eyes.

"After dinner, I'll show you to your room," Violet said to her. She then lifted a hand toward the stove. "This is Lupita. She takes care of us all."

"Hola," the woman greeted her.

Kendra smiled. *"Hola, Lupita. Por favor llámeme Kendra."*

"You speak Spanish!" Lupita returned with a wide grin.

Apparently, she did, but she couldn't think where or how she'd learned. "A little," she murmured self-consciously.

"More than a little, I'd say," Violet commented. "Maybe you can help Lupita dish up while I set the table in the dining room and Maddie makes sure Darcy gets her homework finished before her dad comes for her."

"I'd be glad to," Kendra said, moving toward the stove, from which delicious smells animated. One she recognized. "Fried okra."

"*Sí,* Señorita Kendra. It is one of Jack's favorites."

"It's one of my favorites, too," Kendra said, but then she knew that was not quite right. It was the favorite of someone else, someone close to her, but when she tried to think who it could be, she got nothing. Shaking away the troubling thought, she took the slotted spoon that Lupita offered her and began dipping out the crisp, golden rounds from the fat simmering in a large cast-iron skillet on the stove. "You use a combination of cornmeal and flour for the breading, I see," she noted.

"But dip the cut okra in egg first," Lupita confirmed with a pleased nod.

"I do the same," Kendra murmured, wondering how she could know these small things about herself and not know the important ones.

Swallowing, she concentrated on frying the next batch of okra while Lupita forked a stack of ham steaks onto a platter and began making gravy. Checking the other pots on the stove, Kendra found green beans and boiled potatoes.

"Should the potatoes be mashed?" she asked Lupita.

"Yes. I use the electric mixer on the counter. Milk and butter in the refrigerator."

Setting to work, Kendra drained the potatoes, added the milk and butter and whipped the lot into a thick, creamy consistency. As she turned the creamed potatoes into the serving bowl that Lupita set out for her, she heard heavy footsteps behind her, then Jack asked, "What are you doing?"

She glanced over her shoulder then back to the objects in her hand. Wasn't it obvious?

"Miss Kendra knows her way around the kitchen," Lupita announced proudly, but a glance showed Kendra that Jack's frown had only deepened.

"She's not here to work."

Baffled, Kendra set down the pot in which she'd mixed the potatoes and pivoted around. "Why shouldn't I help out? What else am I going to do? I certainly don't want to sit around all day worrying about what I can't remember."

Jack grimaced then pointed to the bandage on her head. "Don't forget that you're still injured."

She lifted a hand to lightly finger the adhesive bandage. "This is minor. It doesn't even hurt."

"It did enough damage to cause amnesia," he grumbled. "That's not what I call minor."

Aware of Lupita's interested gaze avidly moving back and forth between them, Kendra nodded. "I'll keep that in mind."

Jack just looked at her, his hands sweeping from the side pockets of his jeans to his back pockets, as if they couldn't quite decide where to light. Then his gaze fell on the platter of ham steaks waiting on the island. Without a word, he picked it up and carried it out of the room. Kendra turned back to the chore at hand, only to find Lupita leaning to one side in order to send a look around her to Maddie, her eyebrows slowly lifting.

"What?" Kendra couldn't help asking. Lupita just folded her hands, a blank look on her face. Kendra turned to Maddie, but she, too, had put on a bland expression.

"Oh, nothing," Maddie said. "I've just never seen Jack carry food to the table before."

Lupita snorted. "He sits, he eats, he leaves."

Kendra didn't know what to say to that or if it even warranted comment. After all, he wouldn't have carried that platter just to keep her from doing it. Would he?

Ty Garland, the ranch foreman, came for Darcy just as the family began gathering around the long plank table in the dining room. The girl turned out to be his daughter, and from the way he and Maddie interacted, Kendra deduced that they were romantically involved. Maddie introduced Ty to Kendra then urged him to stay for the meal. He acquiesced readily, before disappearing into the hallway to "wash up." Maddie followed, and Kendra could hear Jack grinding his teeth as they waited for the pair to return. Darcy giggled when they reappeared, holding hands and smiling at each other. Clearing his throat, Ty folded his tall frame into the chair beside Darcy. Maddie took the seat on the girl's other side.

Kendra automatically bowed her head. Beside her, Violet did the same. Jack sat at the end of the table. After a moment, he began to speak the blessing.

"Lord, we thank You for the bounty of this land that feeds us, and for all those, past and present, whose labor blesses us. Keep us ever mindful of Your tender mercies and generosity." He paused briefly then added, "And heal Mom. Please let her come back to us soon. Oh, and help our guest get her memory back and everything squared away. In Jesus's name, amen."

Kendra quietly thanked him for including her in the prayer. She wanted to ask what was wrong with his mother, but she didn't want to pry. Perhaps she could ask later in private. As the food passed and plates piled high, Maddie began to fill in Ty on Darcy's day. The girl had apparently just started school. He listened quietly, occasionally nodding his head and smiling. Once, he reached over and patted Darcy's hand. The girl paused eating long enough to beam a smile up at him. Maddie went on to say that she'd talked to her "other boss" about doing a regular column on the school.

Violet mentioned that Maddie worked part-time at the local newspaper, as well as taking care of Darcy. Talk then turned to a brand of shirts that both Violet and Maddie liked. A certain style had apparently gone on sale. Obviously pleased, Maddie said she'd take a look the following morning.

"I hope they still have that turquoise plaid," Violet mused. "If they do, will you get one for me? I'll pay you back."

"Sure, which one do you prefer, the one with gold thread or silver?"

Violet waved a hand dismissively. "You get one, I'll get the other. Then we can trade as we like."

"My thought exactly." Maddie's eyes twinkled.

Kendra smiled, intrigued and a little envious of the two. She didn't know if she had a sibling. "It must be fun being twins."

"You know, it kind of is," Maddie said, grinning at Violet.

Jack dropped his fork with a *clunk.* "I don't know what's fun about it," he snapped. "I'm not sure I even want to meet my so-called brother."

Kendra gasped. She'd give anything to know if she had family somewhere, anyone at all, really, even a great-aunt or second cousin. While little Darcy watched avidly, Violet and Maddie exchanged troubled looks. Ty stilled as if waiting for Jack to say more, but he did not look up from his plate. After a moment, Jack picked up his fork again and started to eat. The rest of the meal passed in silence.

Kendra found that her appetite had fled with his words. She wondered what she'd walked into here—an ill mother, twins who had never met… She found it all very confusing.

Jack excused himself and left the table without so much as a glance in Kendra's direction. She worried that he might be angry with her. Perhaps they all were. She looked to Violet, on the verge of an apology, but the other woman beat her to it.

"I'm sorry, Kendra. Don't mind Jack. He's got a lot on his mind right now."

"We all do," Maddie added.

"You see," Violet went on, "Jack and I didn't even know until a couple months ago that Maddie, Grayson and our other brother Carter existed."

Kendra switched her shocked gaze back and forth between Violet and Maddie. "How…?" She bit off the question, fearing that to voice it would be rude.

"We don't know," Maddie said flatly.

"And until our mother wakes up…" Violet began.

"Or we find our father," Maddie supplied.

"We won't know why they split the family and raised us apart," Violet finished.

Kendra shook her head, overwhelmed. "That's… that's…" She swallowed the word *awful,* a question occurring. "You said, until your mother wakes up?"

Violet's whole countenance fell. "Mom's in a coma," she whispered. "She fell off her horse."

"Oh, wow," Kendra said, impulsively clasping Violet's hand with hers. "I'm so sorry. I didn't know…."

"No reason why you should," Violet told her, squeezing her hand.

Kendra took her hand back, exclaiming, "I shouldn't be here! You have enough troubles without me bringing mine into the mix."

Both Maddie and Violet rushed to reassure her.

"No, no," Violet said. "It's no bother."

"It might even be a good thing," Maddie said at

the same time. Ty cleared his throat, and she instantly subsided. Kendra could only wonder what that might be about, but she had no time to ponder the matter as Violet suddenly rose.

"You must be tired," she said, "after everything you've been through. Let me show you to your room."

"I'd like to help clean up first," Kendra insisted, aware that she really had no choice but to stay the night here at least.

Violet waved that away. "Lupita will have cleaned up everything but what you see here."

"Ty and I will clear the table and load these things into the dishwasher," Maddie volunteered. Ty lifted an eyebrow but said not a word. He was certainly a quiet type, good-looking, too, almost as good-looking as Jack.

Kendra got up. Suddenly exhausted, she felt herself sway. Violet instantly reached out.

"You poor thing! You haven't recovered at all."

"I'm fine," Kendra said with a wan smile, "just a little tired is all." Straightening, she lifted her chin and took a deep breath.

"You come on with me now," Violet instructed, taking Kendra by the arm.

"Do you have any things to be brought in?" Maddie asked, looking to Ty.

"I left a bag of toiletries in Jack's truck," Kendra said, just then remembering. "Other than that, I only have what I'm wearing."

"I'll run out and get the bag," Maddie told her, hurrying away from the table. "Then I have some things you can borrow."

"We'll get you all fixed up," Violet promised.

Embarrassed, Kendra could do nothing but smile and follow her hostess from the room.

Chapter Four

Violet led Kendra into the living room, a large space beautifully decorated with overstuffed leather pieces and Native American fabrics. They crossed the floor to a sort of open hallway, from which a pair of identical stairways ascended to the second floor from opposite sides of the house. Kendra gazed through a wall of windows to an enclosed courtyard until the stairs turned. They came out on a narrow landing above.

"You'll be just at the head of the stairs," Violet explained, "and I'm at the other end of this landing." She opened a door for Kendra, saying, "Make yourself at home. I'll just run and grab some things for you and be right back."

Kendra wandered into a spacious room with sage-green walls and cream-colored woodwork and carpet. A queen-size bed with a tall, wrought-iron headboard stood against the center of the far wall, its silky, quilted bedspread echoing the sage-and-cream palette with strips of coral pink highlighting the geometric pattern. Marble-topped wrought-iron tables flanked the bed, each holding an identical pottery lamp. A pair of deep window seats, framed by coral-pink drapes and strewn with fluffy pillows, centered each of the side walls, one looking out over the compound, the other over the courtyard below. A small desk and an overstuffed chair in a complementary flower print comprised the only other furnishings, giving the room a clean, airy feel.

Violet returned, her arms full of clothing, the plastic bag of toiletries and the bridal veil, which she dumped on the bed. "Shorts and tops," she announced, "and a few other essentials. The closet is through the bathroom." She pointed to a door beside the one through which she had just entered. "Let me know if you need anything else."

"Thank you. You've all been very kind."

"It's no problem," Violet told her in her soft drawl. "Do you mind if I ask how you came to meet my brother?"

"I'm told that he came on the accident right after it happened and called for help."

"I see. Funny, he never mentioned that part."

"The first time I remember seeing him was when I woke up at the clinic yesterday." Kendra looked inward, remembering that moment. He had seemed so familiar, and yet she hadn't known him—or anyone. "At first, I thought he must be someone connected to me personally. But then I realized that wasn't the case."

"It must be so awful to lose your memory," Violet said, shaking her head. "You don't remember your family, even?"

"No."

"A boyfriend?"

"No one," Kendra said solemnly.

Violet dithered for a moment before saying, "There is that bridal veil."

Kendra closed her eyes. "I don't remember anything about that. Jack says I was wearing it when he found me, but…" She waved a hand at her casual clothing. "That doesn't make any sense. Nothing makes any sense."

"Well, don't you fret about it now," Violet advised, patting her shoulder. "We'll pray on it, and it'll all come back to you."

Kendra nodded, doing her best to smile, but she couldn't be quite so certain as Violet sounded. What if she never figured out who she was or where she belonged? What if she'd run away from an ugly past?

She shook her head, thanked Violet again and watched the other woman leave the room.

"Now you rest," Violet said, gently closing the door behind her.

Kendra stood for a long moment, feeling so very alone.

Oh, Lord, why is this happening to me? What if

my memory never returns? What will happen to me? As kind as they had been, she couldn't expect Jack's family to offer her shelter forever. *Please return my memories to me, and please don't let there be anything in my past to shame You or me.*

She ended her prayer a few minutes later, and once again loneliness swamped her. Desperate to shake it off, she grabbed the plastic bag of toiletries and carried them into the bathroom. Creamy white with splashes of sage and coral, it offered ample storage, a small shower and a lovely tub. The closet had built-in drawers, where she stowed her borrowed clothing and the puzzling veil. Picking out a pair of soft knit shorts and a sleeveless top that could be worn as pajamas, she decided to run a tub of water and take a long, hot soak.

Finding bath salts in a pretty container on the side of the tub, she poured some into the steaming water before taking fluffy towels from a stack in the small linen cabinet. Making a note to get some rubber bands and clips for her hair, she twisted it up inside one of the towels and slid into the steaming water. A pleasant lethargy invaded her tired muscles, and she became aware of soreness in places she hadn't realized had been strained, but she couldn't quite seem to relax. She simply had too many questions circulating around and around in her mind.

The sun had set when she returned to the bedroom in her borrowed pjs. She sat in the window seat, staring down at the softly lit courtyard, trying not to cry. This was a beautiful place, and these were kind people, but this was not *her* place and these were not *her* people. Where did she belong? she wondered. With whom did she belong? And what if she never remembered?

Laying her head back against the wall, she whispered, "What is to become of me?"

She thought suddenly of Jack, of seeing his handsome face when she awoke at the clinic. The urge to talk to him came over her, but she shook her head, determined not to impose. She couldn't cling to a man just because he'd been kind to her, no matter how handsome he was. Besides, Jack seemed to have enough troubles of his own. He didn't need—or likely want—hers added to the heap. Curling into the window seat, she sighed and prepared to endure a long, lonely evening. She could only pray that it would not be a harbinger of evenings to come for the rest of her life.

The peace of early morning slowly invaded Jack's troubled soul as he sipped from his coffee mug. The weather held a hint of fall at dawn, though he knew that the sun would blaze later in the day. Sitting in a comfortably cushioned chair beneath a spreading oak tree at the very edge of the courtyard, he let the coffee do its work and mentally went over his plans for the day.

He still hadn't finished riding fence on the Franken Road section, and the boys had quarantined some cows that seemed to have a worm infestation. Some question existed as to the specific pest, and he needed to try to figure that out today, so he'd probably be taking a sample to the vet over in Wichita Falls. First, though, he had to feed all the animals in the barn.

Normally, Violet handled the farm, pecan grove and vegetable stand in town, Jack tended the ranch and cattle and their mother usually took care of the finances and the livestock at the compound. With Belle out of commission, however, Jack had taken over many of her duties. He wondered how much longer that would be the case. Unfortunately, when he'd called the nursing home before heading down to breakfast this morning, the charge nurse had told him that nothing had changed.

He closed his eyes, remembering with a pang the day that his mother had fallen. The argument had started at breakfast with Jack demanding to know why she objected so vociferously to answering his questions about the past. Growing up, he'd realized that other kids had fathers and grandparents, aunts, cousins…whole family trees. All he and Violet had ever had was their mother's terse assertion that "knowing wouldn't make any difference."

She had ridden out to where he was working with a thermos of iced tea in an attempt to make peace, but he'd been stewing all morning that fateful day. *"How,"* Jack had demanded, following her back to her horse, *"could knowing my father's full name* not *make any difference?"*

"Jack, drop this," Belle had pleaded. *"Trust me when I tell you that you're better off not knowing."*

"How can I be better off not knowing my father or my grandparents?"

"Your grandparents are dead, Jack. You can't blame me for not knowing them!"

"But there has to be other family," Jack had insisted.

Belle had blown up at him then, throwing up her arms and bawling at him. *"All I've ever done is protect and provide for you and your sister! Don't you think that if I could give you more than I have, I would?"*

"I don't know, Mother," Jack had responded coldly. *"Would you?"*

He had seen that he'd hurt her, but he'd closed his heart to her pain, determined to get some concrete answers for once.

"How dare you?" she'd breathed, gathering her reins into her hand. Sensing her distress, her grulla mare, Mouse, had shied, but Belle, an experienced horsewoman, had ignored the animal's nervousness. *"I gave up everything for you and your sister!"* she'd declared. *"And all you can do is complain that it isn't enough!"*

"So tell me, Mom," Jack had harangued, *"what exactly did you give up? And why?"* She hadn't answered him as she'd calmed the horse with a quiet

touch. *"Has it occurred to you that whatever you gave up, Violet and I were forced to give up, too?"* he'd shot at her.

"Yes!" Belle had cried, throwing herself up into the saddle. *"Of course I've thought of that, but I had no choice except to let it happen that way."*

"But why?" he'd demanded.

"I can't tell you that," she'd insisted.

He'd watched helplessly as she'd wheeled the horse and ridden away. Grinding his teeth, he had stamped his foot like a spoiled child as Mouse had stretched out with her long, graceful legs, racing across the ground. Belle and the horse were just tiny figures in the distance when suddenly the horse had stumbled, going to its knees. Jack remembered all too well the horror he'd felt as Belle had sailed over the horse's head. He'd yanked out his cell phone and called for help even as he'd begun to run toward her. Thankfully, Doc had been close by that day, but Jack would never forget seeing his mother lying there in a crumpled heap, her head bent forward beneath her. She'd been in a coma ever since.

God, forgive me, and heal my mother. Please, please bring her back to us. I'll never ask her another question about the past, I promise.

Sucking in a deep breath, he opened his eyes—and saw Kendra slip out of the living-room door into the courtyard. She wore the same shoes and jeans as the day before, but this time she wore a dark blue tank top beneath one of Violet's chambray work shirts, the tail of which she'd tied in a knot at her waist. She'd rolled the sleeves, which were probably too short for her, to her elbows. Her long, golden hair waved buoyantly from a casual center part to flow across her shoulders.

She looked beautiful, achingly so, without a bit of makeup or artifice. Glancing around at the cool, terra-cotta tiling and outdoor furniture scattered about in groupings beneath hanging plants, she jammed her hands into her pockets and wandered deeper into the courtyard. Jack kept expecting her to spot him, but he must have sat too deeply in the shadow of the oak.

Drawing to a stop, she turned her face upward and prayed, "Father, I'm so confused and frightened. I have nowhere to go, nothing to do, not a cent to my name… What is to become of me?"

Jack didn't have answers for her, but he felt compelled to let her know of his presence, so when she said nothing more, he chose an obvious topic and spoke up.

"Sleep okay last night?"

She jerked, her gaze targeting the tree. After a moment, she began to saunter slowly toward him. "Actually, I did. I had some weird dreams, but I can't recall much about them now, and I do feel rested."

"That's good," he said, adding offhandedly, "are you usually such an early riser?" Too late, he realized the futility of asking such a question.

Wincing, she sighed. "I wish I knew."

"Sorry. Should've thought before I spoke." That seemed to be a real problem with him lately.

"It's not your fault," she told him.

She, of course, didn't know about his temper, and he found that he didn't really want her to know. He decided to change the subject.

"How's your head?"

"My head?" Her hand lifted to the bandage on her forehead. "It's fine. I don't even remember it's there most of the time."

"That's good." Lifting his mug, he said, "Lupita won't start breakfast for another hour or so, but there's coffee in the kitchen, if you're interested."

"Maybe later," she told him, gesturing at a chair near his. He waved a hand and shrugged to let her know that she could sit anywhere she liked. She sank down, rubbing her hands over her thighs and knees. "Your sisters are wonderful."

Jack nodded. "Violet's always had a heart of gold," he said. "Hard worker, too."

"And Maddie?"

He looked into his cup. "Maddie has been surprisingly good for Darcy and Ty," he said carefully, "and Violet's thrilled to have found her."

"But not you," Kendra surmised, tilting her head.

Jack shifted in his seat. "I didn't say that. It's just that I didn't grow up with Maddie, and she's not my twin."

"But she is your sister."

"Yes, she is my sister. Her resemblance to Violet proves that."

"What I wouldn't give to discover family. You're so blessed to have found Maddie and Grayson and… I'm sorry. I forget the other name." She shook her head as if to say that had become par for the course.

"Carter," Jack supplied. "He's overseas in the military. If Brian Wallace is my father, then Carter is my half brother."

"If?" she echoed. "But I thought—"

"Doesn't matter," he interrupted, tossing out the last of his coffee. He put the cup on the ground and got up. "To tell you the truth, I don't even want to know if Brian is my father or not."

"How can you say that?" she whispered, clearly mystified.

He lifted a hand to forestall more questions. How had they even gotten on this subject? "I have to feed the stock."

"Oh," she said, sounding forlorn.

Jack tried very hard to just walk away, but somehow he couldn't, not without growling, "You can come along if you want."

She perked up instantly, bouncing to her feet. "Okay. Sure."

Jack turned away, striking out for the barn. She quickly fell in beside him. They walked along a pavestone path to the back gate in the wrought-iron fence. From there, the path became more of a bare rut worn in the grass by the passing of many feet.

The dog, Nipper, loped across the field to join them. Without slowing his stride, Jack bent to ruffle the dog's shaggy fur. As they drew closer to the barn, the dog peeled off and loped away.

After a moment, Jack glanced at Kendra. "You're not alone, you know. You're among friends here, and just because you don't remember, doesn't mean that someone somewhere isn't missing you."

"Do you really think so?"

"I'd guess that you have a fiancé worrying about you, at the very least," he said. He'd come to that conclusion at some point during the night, despite having made every effort *not* to think about her.

She held up her hand. "If that's true, why don't I have a ring?"

He shook his head. "Don't know. But there is that veil."

She flapped her hands in agitation. "It's maddening not to be able to remember!"

"Funny, isn't it?" he murmured. "You know far less about your past than you want to. And now I know more about mine than I want to."

Not long ago, he'd been desperate to know all the secrets of his past, but since his mom's accident, he'd gladly forget everything he'd come to know if he could just have Belle back, safe and sound.

"What am I going to do with you?" Jack said, patting the dark red hide of the Hereford calf. "Why aren't you drinking water?"

"Have you tried warming it?" Kendra heard herself ask.

"Warming the water? We warm formula when we bottle-feed, but I've never heard of warming the water."

Kendra shrugged, feeling certain that her suggestion would help but without knowing why. "Can't hurt to try, right?"

"We have a sink over here," he said thoughtfully, picking up the water bucket. He tossed the cool water, and she followed him to a small room tucked into the front corner of the huge barn. He lifted the plastic bucket into the deep metal sink and turned on the spigot. "How warm do you think it ought to be?"

"It should feel fairly warm to the touch," she answered, still wondering how she knew these things.

A yellow-striped cat appeared from behind a pile of feed sacks.

"Hello, there." Kendra went to her knees on the straw-strewn floor. "Oh, look, she's going to have kittens."

"No way."

"Way. What's her name?"

"Tom," he answered wryly.

"Tomasina, maybe," Kendra chortled.

He shut off the faucet and lifted the full bucket from the sink, placing it on the ground next to the cat. Squatting, he reached out with his square, long-fingered hands and turned the cat onto its back.

"Well, I'll be. She is pregnant."

Jack rested his forearms across his thighs and looked her in the face. “How do you know these things?”

“I just do,” she told him helplessly. “Don’t ask me where I learned such things, though, because I have no idea.”

“Let’s see what else you know,” he said, pushing up to his feet and snagging the handle of the water bucket.

She trailed him at a safe distance while he swiftly carried the sloshing bucket back to the stall where the calf waited. Jack lifted the bucket over the stall gate and set it on the ground. The calf nosed the pail, swished its tail and started to drink. Turning his pale brown eyes on Kendra, Jack tilted his head. “Wouldn’t have believed it if I hadn’t seen it.”

“Try giving him a warm pail every morning for the next week or so,” Kendra said. “He ought to be well hydrated and less picky by then.”

Jack stared at her for so long that Kendra blushed. “Come with me.” He waved her along as he strode down the aisle between the pens. “What do you know about goats?”

“This breed gives exceptional milk, good for cheese,” she said, looking at the kid nestled in the hay. “Forages well in conjunction with cattle.”

Jack promptly strode off again, coming to a stop seconds later in front of a pigsty that opened into a sizable outdoor pen. “What’s the difference in a pig and a hog?”

"A hog's just a pig that weighs more than a hundred and twenty-five pounds."

Off Jack went again, leading her past half a dozen stalls with horses and out the back of the barn to a small, fenced chicken yard, where he eyed her pointedly.

Kendra glanced over the pen and said, "You've got some good-looking Leghorns here."

Pointing to another nearby pen with a plastic pond set in the ground, Jack asked, "What do you make of those?"

"You mean those white mallard hatchlings?"

Jack folded his arms, legs braced wide apart. "You either grew up on a farm or…"

"Or what?"

He shook his head. "You know a lot about animals, that's all."

"I guess I do," she said, lifting the top on a hinged plastic bin of cracked corn. She used the scoop inside to pour feed into a chute that spilled into a shallow trough inside the chicken pen. She dumped in a second scoop and closed the lid.

"That's exactly the right amount of feed," Jack told her, clearly impressed. Then he nodded toward the feed bin. "Want to feed the ducks, too?"

"Not corn," she said automatically. "Got any barley?"

Smiling, he pointed to another bin beside the barn door. "You're definitely a farm girl."

"Maybe," she muttered. "Wish I knew."

Shrugging, she fed the ducks, making sure to toss some of the barley pellets into the water. For several moments, they watched adult ducks launch into the artificial pond and feed while the hatchlings pecked the pellets off the ground.

"How much longer before you turn them out?" she asked.

"In another couple days, we'll start opening the gate for them in the morning. They'll return on their own in the evening, and we'll close them in for the night. Otherwise the coyotes pick 'em off."

"Sensible."

"We think so." He led her around to the side of the barn to check on and feed the pregnant heifer in the corral there before going back into the barn to take care of the horses.

"I can help with that," she informed him.

He shot her a crooked smile. "Not surprised. You figure you ride?"

"I don't know," she answered, looking over the animals in the stalls. "If I did, though, I'd choose this mouse grulla. What a beauty!"

Jack's frown surprised her. "You stay away from that horse," he said flatly, even as the grulla nosed Kendra's palm through the metal pipes of the stall gate.

"Why? Is she—"

"Just stay away from her," he ordered, turning his back on her.

Puzzled, Kendra petted the mare's velvety nose

before quickly following Jack down the aisle between the stalls. He showed her where to find the feed and the water controls for each stall.

"I know you must have more horses than these," Kendra remarked as they worked to clean the stalls and feed the animals.

"We do," he replied. "These are just our personal stock. We run two full strings of working stock besides."

"A string would be twenty head?"

"That's right."

"Whose mare is that about to foal back there in the last stall?"

"The bay is no one's personal mount. I bought her from a guy who thought she was ill. Neither of us realized she was foaling out of season until I got her home and the vet got a look at her."

Kendra nodded. "Happens that way sometimes, but not often."

"So I'm told. Now, I'm wondering who told you."

She couldn't do anything but sigh and shake her head. "Haven't got a clue."

Keeping one hand on the sorrel in the stall that they were currently cleaning, Kendra slowly walked around the horse, knowing that it was less likely to kick her if it knew where she was at all times.

"You may not ride, but you definitely know your way around a horse," Jack commented, watching her.

A voice hailed them from the front of the building. "Hello!"

"Back here," Jack called.

As the Grasslands sheriff joined them, Kendra tensed, fearing what he might have to tell her. She desperately wanted to know who she was and all that she'd forgotten, but at the same time, she feared what that might be. Was she a car thief on the lam? Had she left behind people who loved and missed her or only enemies and cohorts in crime?

Chapter Five

"What have you found out?" Jack asked, seeming as tense as Kendra felt.

"Not a thing," the sheriff answered. "There's no record that the car has ever been tagged, titled or even assigned to a dealer in the whole state." He looked to Kendra, adding, "I've got nothing on you, either."

Kendra swayed, weak with relief—until she realized all that meant. She might not be a car thief, but no one had reported her missing, apparently.

Swallowing, she asked, "So what now?"

The law waved a hand. "I've got no reason to hold you here any longer. You're free to leave anytime you want."

And go where?

Jack spoke up. "Doc wants her to stay around until her stitches come out."

"That's between y'all and the doc," George retorted.

Jack looked at her, saying carefully, "Kendra will stay here till Doc's through with her, then."

She breathed a silent sigh of relief, offering him a wobbly smile. That gave her a little over a week to get her memory back or figure out where to go next.

"Kendra?" George exclaimed, hooking his thumbs in his gun belt.

"It's a made-up name," Jack explained quickly. "Little girl at the clinic decided it suited her. Gotta call her something."

"Guess 'Hey, you' is out of the question," George chortled.

Kendra winced at the careless remark, and Jack tucked his chin and glared at the sheriff from beneath the dark slashes of his eyebrows until George cleared his throat.

"Well, I'll be getting along," he muttered.

"Thanks for coming out," Jack said.

"No problem. Thought I'd deliver the good news in person."

Jack glanced at Kendra then nodded at George and waved a hand in farewell. The sheriff strolled away. As soon as he was out of earshot, Kendra mumbled, "Good news?"

Jack reached out a hand and gently cupped her shoulder. "George means no harm. I guess from his perspective, it's good news that you're not wanted for car theft or something."

She blurted, "But what if I *am* a car thief? Or worse!"

Jack shook his head, a lopsided smile in place. "Nah. A girl who knows her ducks and chickens is salt of the earth."

Smiling wanly, Kendra glanced around. "Well, at least I can help out around here."

Jack took hold of his pitchfork again. "Let's wrap this up, then, so we can grab some grub."

Kendra went to work, but in the back of her mind hovered the thought that she had only a little over a week left here. All she could do in the meantime was pray that her memory would return before she had to go.

While making quick work of breakfast, Jack tried to turn his mind to the day's chores, but his keen awareness of Kendra's mood constantly drew his mind back to her predicament. Pensive and morose, she did little more than push food around on her plate and sip at her coffee. He couldn't help wondering what she would do with herself that day. She had seemed alternately relieved and distraught about George's news—or rather the lack of it—and Jack could tell that her situation preyed on her mind now.

Whenever he felt overburdened, he headed over to the old Lindley house and went to work refurbishing the place. Keeping busy occupied his mind and held worry at bay. He would hate to be stuck in a strange place with nothing to do all day. Having come to that conclusion, he couldn't very well walk out and leave her sitting there to stew.

Draining the last little bit of his coffee, he pushed back his chair. He then all but dropped his mug onto the table and, as casually as possible, asked, "Want to ride along with me today?"

She looked surprised, but then she offered him a soft smile and a gentle nod. "Yes, thank you."

He shrugged, getting to his feet. "Nothing exciting going on. It'll beat sitting around here twiddling your thumbs, though."

Popping up from her chair, she looked down at herself, smoothing her hands over her slender middle. "Should I change?"

'No, you're fine," he answered, looking away. She was more than fine, actually. She was breathtaking. He suddenly wished he'd kept his mouth shut, but it was too late to withdraw the invitation.

He told Lupita not to expect them for lunch then headed down the hall. Kendra followed him, pausing while he grabbed his hat from the peg on the wall then trailing him out to his truck. They rode in near silence along the ranch trail to the gathering pen where the hands had bunched the cattle.

His uncle James had built the pen, an old-fashioned, wood-plank corral with weathered square posts, in a rolling landscape of tall grass, which had turned gold at the top, leaving only the bottoms of the slender reeds green. Barbed-wire fencing stitched the pastures together into a crazy quilt of range, hemmed on two sides by lines of trees still darkly leafed, their trunks the color of charcoal. The crumbling chute of the corral had been replaced with a portable one made of pipe, its red paint now chipped and rough. Jack had always like this spot and knew that the remains of an old line shack from the day of the open range could be found just over the rise to the east. Jack had often poked around there while James had performed what was now his own job. He felt very blessed in that moment to be doing what he was doing in this lush place.

Looking to the woman next to him, he said, "You can sit in the truck if you want."

She shook her head and let herself out of the cab. Nevertheless, she held back while he strode over and climbed up on the corral fence.

"Is this all of them?" he asked.

"Near as we can tell," Ty answered, wading through a chest-high bovine sea. "I'd say it's a virus."

"But we wormed as usual this year," Jack pointed out.

"We did," Ty agreed. "If I didn't know better, I'd think it was lung worms because of the coughs."

"Lung worms!" Jack retorted. "Is there a swamp around here I don't know about? This is northwest Texas, and in case you've missed it, we've been in drought much of the year." He'd only seen lung worms once in his lifetime, and his uncle James had declared it the wettest year on record.

Ty shrugged. "The vet's going to have to tell us, then, because I'm all out of ideas. We treated for parasites when we first noticed we could have a problem."

"Did the coughs start before or after you treated for parasites?" Kendra asked.

Jack glanced at her in surprise. Shading her eyes with her hand, she looked calmly up at him. She'd asked a very prescient question, one he wouldn't have thought to ask himself.

"Are you thinking the cattle could have been poisoned by the insecticide?"

She dropped her hand, staring into the distance for several seconds before murmuring, "I've seen cards."

"Cards?"

She looked up at him then. "Uh, like, I don't know, flash cards or reference cards. I—I remember one about grubs."

"Grubs?" Ty echoed skeptically. "Like grub worms?"

"You might know them as warbles or cattle wolves."

Ty lifted his eyebrows and shot a thoughtful look at Jack. "Warbles could produce these symptoms if they got into the cow's esophagus."

Jack braced an elbow against the top rail of the corral fence and addressed Kendra frankly. "How do we find out for sure?"

She shrugged uncomfortably. "Well, I suppose you have to take samples and get them to a lab."

That was pretty much what the vet had said.

“Hang on while I call Anderson,” Jack said to his foreman. Taking out his phone, he dialed the crusty, overworked veterinarian and after some time, finally got through to him. A short conversation followed. Afterward, Jack addressed Ty, detailing what needed to be done.

Ty shook his head. “We have to comb the cattle,” he said. “Seriously? With what, exactly?”

Glancing around, Kendra asked, “Anyone have a pocket comb?”

One of the hands reluctantly dug into a hip pocket. “I’ll buy you a new one,” Jack promised.

“Aw, he’s got lots of spares,” another cowboy joked. “I always figured that the number of combs a fellow owns is indicative of his level of vanity.”

“Well, it’s for sure you don’t have any,” the first man retorted, “because you’ve got nothing to be vain about.”

“All right, all right,” Ty said over the laughter. “We’ve got work to do. I’ve got zippered bags in my truck. One of you go get ’em.”

“The rest of you haze one of the sickest heads into the chute,” Jack said, climbing up onto the fence.

Kendra interrupted with a quiet comment. “You ought to wear gloves.”

Jack pulled his leather work gloves from the waistband of his jeans.

“Disposable gloves,” she corrected, “to prevent cross-contamination of the samples.”

“Sugar, this ain’t no hospital,” Jack quipped drily.

"We don't keep disposable gloves out on the range, you know."

"Then a different person needs to gather samples from each of the cattle."

"We don't have enough men for that." Ty nodded at the hundred or so head of cattle shifting about the pen.

"Anderson said we only need to pick out a few of the sickest ones, so long as it's an odd number..." Jack said.

"I can take the first sample," Kendra volunteered, coming forward to climb up onto the fence with him.

"Do you know how to do that?" Jack asked.

Blinking, she seemed to be running through steps in her mind. "I—I'm not sure I've ever actually done it, but I know how. I think."

Jack shrugged. "Well, if you're willing to get your hands dirty..."

She surprised him by smiling and saying, "I don't mind."

Jack shared a look with Ty, who seemed as impressed as Jack himself. Belle and, to a slightly lesser extent, Violet, were the only other two women of Jack's acquaintance who would willingly do the dirty work on the ranch. Ty had remarked more than once that ownership of a ranch made the obvious difference, but did that mean Kendra owned or perhaps worked a ranch somewhere? If so, that would explain a lot. Jack smiled despite even himself.

Clearing his throat, Jack put on a serious face. "Let's get to it."

They climbed over the fence. Kendra stepped down to the ground an instant after he did. He noticed that she stayed right behind him as he cut a swath through the milling herd to the chute. She studied her options for a moment then picked a spot where she could easily reach through the pipes near the head of the cow. Reaching behind her, she gathered her long hair into a tail at the nape of her neck and literally tied it in a knot to hold it back out of her way. As soon as she bent forward, it slid free and fell about her face. One of the hands passed Jack a folded bandanna, which he shook out and offered to her.

Smiling her thanks, she quickly rolled the bandanna into a long strip and tied back her hair. The white square bandage on her forehead caught his eye, and Jack suddenly wondered if she ought to be out here like this. But she took her place again, and he knew it was too late to argue with her about it. Irked by his thoughtlessness, he held out his hand for the comb. It slapped into his palm, and he handed it off to Kendra. The boys prodded the yearling that they'd loaded into the narrow passageway of the chute. It moved forward, and she went to work.

"I need bags," she called, crouching to comb the tops of the cow's front legs. "Grubs migrate from the hair around the hooves, up the body," she murmured to herself, depositing hair and tiny wormlike things into the bag before sealing it. "You'll want to record the date, time, cattle ID and where on the body the sample was taken," she said, handing the bag to Jack.

Ty went to get a marker out of his truck while she took another sample from the same cow's upper chest then from around its mouth and head. Jack checked the cow's ear tag and wrote the relevant information on each of three bags.

"That ought to do it," she said, "but we've got to either sterilize this comb or get another."

After some discussion, the men used first-aid kits from both Ty's and Jack's trucks to clean the comb after each of the first two cows. After the third, it went into a trash bag.

Kendra removed the bandanna from her hair, which fell sleek and golden about her shoulders again. She held up the folded scarf, asking, "Whose is this?"

A burly cowhand by the unlikely name of Johnson Parks shyly stepped forward. Kendra offered him a very personal smile and a soft, "Thank you."

Parks turned three shades of red and stammered, "W-w-welcome."

A little irritated by the cowboy's obvious enchantment, Jack busied himself by putting the nine samples into the glove box of his truck. He ordered the men to keep the cattle confined until the lab results came back on the samples and a treatment could be administered, then gruffly told Kendra that it was time to go.

"Let's get some hay out here," Ty ordered.

"Just hay?" Kendra asked Jack as she climbed up into the truck cab. "Not grain, too?"

Jack shook his head. "We sell grass-fed beef. Use antibiotics only on diseased cows. Absolutely no hormones, and no unhealthy proteins."

"I like that." She beamed at him, and he felt the last of his irritation melt away. No wonder Parks acted like a fool around her.

He shut her door and walked around to slide behind the steering wheel. "I'll take you back to the house now."

"Oh," she said, sounding a little disappointed. "Okay."

"Or," he ventured impulsively, "you could just ride over to the lab in Wichita Falls with me. I'll buy you lunch."

"You'll have to," she said with a wide smile. "I don't have a nickel to my name. That I know of."

"You may not know whether you have a bank account or not," he said, starting up the truck, "but you do know a thing or two about animals."

She ducked her head and said, "Thank you," as if he'd complimented her. Maybe he had. Maybe he'd even meant to.

He shifted uncomfortably, muttering, "Buckle up."

Nodding, she secured her seatbelt and then shyly watched him follow suit.

As the truck bounced along the trail to the county road, Kendra looked around her with interest, eventually commenting, "This is beautiful land."

"I've always thought so," Jack said.

"You have a good life here."

"Yes, ma'am," he agreed heartily. "Wouldn't want any other."

"I hope my life is something like this," she said after a few minutes. "Do you think it might be?"

Jack could only speculate. "Well, you seem to know your way around a barn and a pasture. You had to come by that somehow."

She nodded but didn't seem particularly encouraged. "Looks like someone ought to have reported me missing by now, doesn't it?"

He was surprised by that himself, but he said, "It's early days yet. Don't you have to wait at least forty-eight hours before you can report someone missing?"

"Yes, I think so."

"I'll have George check on that."

She seemed to relax a little. "Thank you."

After a while, he popped in a favorite CD, and the cab filled with country-western music. Kendra laughed at one song, an amusing ditty about a man missing his girlfriend after she gave him an ultimatum: choose her or fishing. At least the fish were biting, the artist sang.

"Haven't you heard that song before?" he asked without thinking.

She thought a moment before shaking her head. “I don’t think so.”

“What’s your favorite song?”

She pondered again then bit her lip. “The only songs I can think of are kids’ Christmas songs.”

Jack decided to try another tack. “What’s your favorite color?”

Bracing her elbow on the armrest, she leaned her head against the heel of her hand and concentrated hard. “Orange. Because it’s so cheerful. But there’s something about deep blue velvet…” Straightening, she sighed. “The worst part is not being able to remember people,” she said in a shaky voice. “There has to be someone who misses me, someone I ought to be missing. Doesn’t there?”

“Yeah,” Jack agreed softly. “There does. There is.”

Gulping, she looked away, turning her gaze out the window.

They came up Highway 277 and reached the outskirts of Wichita Falls just about lunchtime after some ninety-plus minutes on the road. Kendra had been silent for much of the trip, and Jack searched for a way to engage her that would lift her mood. Finally, he asked, “What are you in the mood to eat?”

“Whatever,” she told him listlessly. “Suit yourself. But shouldn’t we drop off these samples first?”

“Might as well,” he said, realizing it would only take a few minutes. Doc Anderson had promised to call ahead and let the agricultural lab know they were coming.

Jack made the requisite turns and pulled up in front of the low, nondescript brick building. Reaching into the glove box for the samples, he told Kendra to "sit tight," saying that he'd only be a few minutes. Nodding, she stayed where she was while he trotted inside and dropped off the bags. When he returned, sliding behind the steering wheel with his keys in hand, she stopped him before he could reach the ignition.

"When will the results be ready?"

"Uh, usually takes a day or two."

"No, it doesn't," she said, opening the truck door.

Jack found himself following her into the building. "Are you sure about this?" he asked as she pushed inside.

"Yes," she answered tersely, marching toward the nearest desk.

Jack grabbed her elbow and redirected her to the skinny young man who had taken his samples, which still lay on the corner of his desk.

Literally vibrating with purpose, Kendra managed a smile for the fellow before declaring, "We need those test results today."

The man looked to Jack. "Our turnaround—" he began.

"All you have to do is identify the parasite," Kendra said, cutting him off. "Nine samples, nine slides.

I'm sure they'll all be the same. Put them under the microscope and tell us what it is."

He stared at her for a moment, his gaze gliding over the bandage on her forehead. She stuck her thumbs in the belt loops of her jeans and rocked back on her heels as if prepared to wait right there all day. Jack thought he'd never seen a more magnificent sight. Quiet but in control, soft-spoken but sure. The tech was made of sterner stuff than him if he could deny her.

"Okay," the lab tech relented. "If they're all the same, I can let you know later this afternoon. If there's more than one..."

"Then we'll wait for your full analysis," she conceded gracefully.

The fellow nodded and began jotting instructions on the bags.

Sighing with satisfaction, Kendra spun on her heel and bumped into Jack, who had watched the entire exchange with growing respect and amazement. Taking her by the elbow again, he nodded at the lab tech and escorted Kendra out of the building.

"In all these years," he said, "I've never gotten results from that lab in less than two days."

"This just isn't that difficult," she told him, "and I'm sure you want to settle on a proper treatment as quickly as possible."

He paused as she climbed up onto the passenger seat of the truck cab. Once she was settled, he stated, "I guess it wouldn't do any good to ask how you know any of this."

She released a deep sigh. "It just…comes to me. But that's good, right? I mean, if enough stuff comes back to me, it'll all come back. Won't it?"

He had no idea, so he just smiled, closed the door and hurried around to reclaim the driver's seat.

He chose barbecue for lunch, killing time by driving across the city of some 100,000 residents, almost all the way out to Sheppard Air Force Base. The restaurant had been given a facelift since he'd last been there, with rough siding, a hitching rail and a steep tin roof over a porch scattered with rocking chairs. The place was packed. As usual, the patrons were expected to stand in line to reach the counter and place an order, then pick a table and wait for a server to deliver the food. An open drink station had been added to the dining room.

Kendra ordered first, sliced beef and the sweet sauce, with a salad and pickled beets, of all things.

"Sounds good, doesn't it?" she said before rushing off to go wash up.

Jack had never developed a taste for beets, so he just smiled and watched her go. The man in line behind him nudged him in the back. Stepping forward, Jack ordered sausage with the spiciest barbecue sauce in the house, corn on the cob and green beans. The fellow behind him chuckled and leaned close to comment.

"I'd eat beets, if I was you. I'd eat dirt if a little gal like that wanted me to."

As a server handed over a tray with flatware, plastic tumblers and a plastic sign with a number on it, Jack inclined his head to get a look at the interloper. Broad-shouldered and just a bit soft around the middle, the thirty-something guy wore a gimme cap, a T-shirt two sizes too small and pants at least two sizes too large.

For some reason, Jack felt compelled to say, "She don't mind a little dirt, that's for sure. Why, she helped me work cattle this morning."

His new friend smacked a palm over the rock-band logo on his shirt, declaring, "Be still my heart!" Then the man tapped his brow, asking, "That how she got the bandage on her forehead there?"

"Uh, no. Fender bender."

"Huh. Women drivers. Gotta love 'em, though, right?"

Jack just lifted his brows, nodded his chin and walked over to a booth, standing there until the busboy finished cleaning it up.

Gotta love 'em. Sometimes when you don't even want to, he mused.

Kendra returned from the ladies' room just as he slid the tray onto the table.

"My turn," he said, motioning toward the men's room.

She caught up the dark red plastic tumblers. "I'll get the drinks. What'll you have?"

"Sweet tea. No lemon."

She carried the tumblers over to the drink station.

As Jack strolled across the room, he noticed how the men followed her with their eyes. That gave him a funny feeling in his chest, part pride, part fear. Bandage or no bandage, the woman was a beauty.

But they don't know what I know about her. Then he had to chuckle and shake his head. No one knew anything of any importance about her.

Except, somehow, he did.

He knew that she was a believer, that his lifestyle was not foreign to her, that she loved animals and possessed a fierce intelligence and a horde of knowledge beneath that soft blond exterior. He knew that she wasn't afraid to work and displayed good sense. He knew that she was lost and afraid and needed a champion.

He also knew that he was the last man any sane, sensible girl ought to choose as her rescuer. Yet, if not him, then who? The cowhand, Parks? A beefy guy in a rock 'n' roll T-shirt? Some man from her nebulous past? He didn't much like any of those options, but he knew that it shouldn't be him.

Chapter Six

They got the lab results within the hour. Kendra was right. Cattle grubs, otherwise known as warbles or cattle wolves, had infested the cattle. Jack gaped at Kendra after he got off the phone with the lab tech.

"You were right. You called it."

She couldn't quite believe it herself. Sitting back in the booth at the restaurant, she laughed and shook her head. Then an idea occurred. Lurching forward to bend over the table, she asked, "Have you ever seen cards like I remember? They're like flash cards, with color photos on one side and information on the other." She closed her eyes, picturing the cards. "Um, common, Latin or scientific names, descriptions, seasonal data, treatment options and directions…"

Jack replied, "No, not really. Well… Sometimes at the ranch supply store, where they stock the chemical treatments, they have signs telling you what to use to treat which pest."

She considered that, nodding. "Could be what I'm remembering."

"I've never seen one on cattle grubs, though," he added thoughtfully. "They must be more common wherever you're from."

"Is there a computer I could use to do a little research?" she asked eagerly.

"Sure. I'll loan you my laptop later tonight."

"Thank you."

"No problem. Now, let me call Doc Anderson again."

He contacted the veterinarian on his cell phone and received what amounted to a prescription via text. They left the restaurant and stopped by a large ranch supply store that Jack sometimes used in the city. He produced the text, which contained a bar code that a clerk scanned. After Jack paid, the necessary chemicals were delivered to them, along with detailed instructions for their use.

Kendra could not remember any specific incident from her past that would have caused her to make that mental leap. All she had to hang her suggestion on was the memory of the hand-size card that she'd described to Jack. She sensed that she'd seen others, but she could not remember the details of those. It was maddening, but also exciting. She couldn't wait to get on Jack's computer and see if she could find something to open a crack in the black wall of her past.

Unfortunately, when Jack dropped her back at the

house late in the afternoon, he said nothing about the computer. Neither did he suggest that she accompany him out to the holding pen again. Doing her best not to betray her disappointment, she thanked him for lunch and went into the house to insist on helping Lupita with her remaining chores, despite the other woman's protest.

"If I don't keep busy, I'll worry," Kendra explained.

Lupita gave in, and Kendra occupied herself by helping the woman polish the tile floors then start dinner. Consequently, everything got done early, so the dinner table was laid before Maddie or Violet even came home that evening. Jack walked in through the front door at the last minute, tossing his hat onto the beautiful buffet table and announcing that he had to clean up before he could eat, even though he was "starved." He seemed in a distracted mood, telling the others to start without him.

Kendra expected his sisters to say that they'd wait for him, but instead they bowed their heads. Violet prayed, and they quickly filled their plates. Kendra dithered, placing a spoonful of this on her plate and slowly eating it before reaching for a spoonful of that. Jack returned a long quarter hour later to drop down into his chair and stab a steak with his fork, shifting it from the serving platter to his plate.

His sisters jumped up within seconds after he began to eat.

"Gotta rush," Violet said. "Need to change."

"Landon back in town?" Jack asked, frowning.

Violet sighed. “No. Not yet.”

“This is First Wednesday,” Maddie announced.

“Oh, right.”

They rushed off, and Jack tucked into his food. After a few minutes, Kendra cleared her throat and said, “You mentioned a laptop computer.”

Jack speared a slice of fried potato. “Yeah, I’ll get it for you after I finish eating.”

“Great. Thanks.”

Before that happened, however, Maddie came back into the room. She wore a skirt with a neat little sweater and a cute pair of flat mules. Violet was right behind her in fresh jeans and a clean blouse. She carried a gray-and gold-colored blocked shirt on a hanger, which she thrust at Kendra.

“This is for you.”

Kendra blinked, then smiled. “That’s very kind. Thank you.”

“It’s to wear tonight,” Maddie informed her.

“That’s right,” Violet confirmed. “You’ll go with us, won’t you?”

“Uh, I—I’m not sure. Go where?”

“To church,” Maddie replied. “First Wednesday is a women’s Bible study that’s held before prayer meeting the first Wednesday of every month.”

Kendra thought about the research she wanted to do, but the thought of church in any form suddenly beckoned to her. She nodded. “I’d like that.”

“Okay,” Violet said. “You run up and change. We’ll clear the table.”

Jack paused in the act of spooning the last of the creamed spinach onto his plate and scowled. “Hey, I’m still eating here.”

“So eat,” Violet retorted, picking up the now-empty bowl and the fried-potato platter to carry them from the room. Maddie followed her with the bread basket and steak plate.

“What about the laptop?” Jack asked Kendra as she quickly rose.

“Maybe you could leave it where I can find it?”

He scowled but said, “Guess I can leave it on the breakfast table.”

The sisters returned, Violet carrying a piece of lemon-meringue pie and Maddie a pitcher of tea. They placed both in front of their brother then grinned at Kendra.

“What are you waiting for?”

“I’m going,” she laughed, doing that.

“So what am I supposed to do?” she heard Jack grumble.

She glanced over her shoulder in time to see Violet shoot a look at Maddie before replying, “What you always do, I guess. Hang around here until it’s time for prayer meeting.”

“Maybe I’ll get ten minutes of peace, then,” he grunted.

Sighing impatiently, Violet went to his side, bent, brushed back his hair and smacked a kiss onto his forehead. She looked to Maddie then, and the twins shared a knowing smile. Kendra felt that she had missed something, but she couldn't very well ask what. After all, she was missing her whole life, everything but the last couple days.

She rushed off to change.

The shirt proved to be a little longer than the others that Violet had loaned her, so she tucked in the tail before rolling back the sleeves, which were still too short. Grabbing the hairbrush, she bent at the waist and gave her hair a vigorous stroking, wishing that she had some clips or hair bands with which to style it. She applied a dab of lip gloss then impulsively peeled the bandage from her forehead. The wound looked dry and smooth, the stitches neat and even. She decided to make do with a pair of flesh-colored adhesive bandages. As soon as she walked back into the dining room a few minutes later, Jack's jitters bustled her out of the house and into Violet's small SUV. The twins chortled as they drove away.

"Did you see Jack's face?" Violet asked.

"And our brother says he's sworn off romance," Maddie giggled.

"I don't get it," Kendra admitted, unsure what was being implied.

Violet pinned her with a look via the rearview mirror. "Jack thought he was going to have you to himself for a while tonight."

Kendra felt a spurt of elation, but she ruthlessly tamped it down. The last thing she or Jack needed was a romance. "No…I'm sure you're wrong about that. We were alone together much of the day, after all."

"Oh, really?" Violet crowed.

"A-at the barn this morning," Kendra clarified, "while tending the stock. Then later we drove to Wichita Falls to deliver samples to the lab for testing."

"Wichita Falls!" Maddie exclaimed. "There and back is at least four hours."

"Well, yes," Kendra said. She thought it best not to mention that they'd had lunch, too. "I think you're reading too much into it, though," she went on doggedly. "Jack's manner toward me is completely…" Okay, so he wasn't *entirely* impersonal. "He thinks I'm probably engaged."

Maddie twisted in her seat. "What makes him think so?"

"The wedding veil."

"Oh…right. Forgot about that. But there's engaged and then there's *engaged*."

She looked pointedly to Violet, who grinned and said, "Especially if you're engaged to the wrong man."

Kendra shook her head. "Why do I always feel like I'm missing half the conversation with you two? Must be that twin thing."

Both girls burst out laughing, then Maddie said,

"I was more or less engaged to Violet's fiancé, Landon, when they met."

Kendra gasped. "Oh, my!"

"I wasn't *in love,* though," Maddie explained. "Now I am. In love and engaged. To Ty."

"And so am I," Violet proclaimed, "in love and engaged to marry Landon Derringer, that is." The twins emitted tiny, identical sighs of satisfaction before Violet added, "He's in Fort Worth on business right now, and I sure do miss him."

Kendra sat back in her seat, astounded at these revelations, but one bit of outstanding information had been glossed over. "Why has Jack sworn off romance?"

This time the sighs were much more gusty.

"Her name was Tammy Simmons…" Violet began.

By the time they pulled into the graveled parking lot next to the pretty white church with its elegant steeple, Kendra hurt for Jack and could only be glad that she wouldn't be encountering Tammy Simmons anytime soon. No wonder the poor guy could go from warm to frosty in the blink of an eye. With memories such as those hinted at by Violet, he was bound to have some heavy-duty reflexive barriers that would pop up at the least provocation. She wondered if she might have suffered a similar disappointment. Maybe that was why she had been wearing that veil and driving like a maniac—and why she didn't remember anything that happened before she woke up in the clinic.

Violet and Maddie introduced her to everyone at the meeting simply as Kendra. However, her story had already circulated around the town, and no one seemed shy about asking her questions—no one but a mousy little woman named Sadie Johnson, who sat down next to Kendra just as the opening prayer began. Though grateful for the prayers that were said on her behalf, Kendra couldn't help feeling uncomfortable. Sadie surprised her by offering a timid smile.

"I'm very sorry for what you're suffering through," the church secretary all but whispered.

Kendra noticed that the slight, delicate young woman had chosen to wear oversize clothing. Even her eyeglasses were too large for her.

"Thank you," Kendra softly replied. "It's rather frightening not to remember anything at all about your past."

"I suppose," Sadie murmured, her gaze turning inward. "I sometimes wish I could forget my past."

"Why is that?" Kendra asked, compelled to engage this unassuming girl.

Jolted from her reverie, Sadie suddenly looked down, shrugging. "It's just that I spent a lot of time in foster homes. Seems like I was always moving around from place to place."

"That would be tough," Kendra admitted. "I wonder if I was in foster care. That might explain why I don't remember my family."

"It might," Sadie agreed.

"What was it like?" Kendra asked, excited to think that Sadie's memories might spark her own, but Sadie almost physically withdrew, shaking her head.

"I—I don't like to talk about it."

"Oh, of course. I understand."

The leader, an older woman, claimed everyone's attention then by asking that they turn to the sixteenth chapter of Psalms. Someone handed an extra Bible to Kendra, and she was glad to find that she knew right where to find the passage. The fifth and sixth verses especially spoke to her.

LORD, You alone are my portion and my cup; You make my lot secure. The boundary lines have fallen for me in pleasant places; surely I have a delightful inheritance.

Those verses might have been written specifically for her situation. Who, after all, did she ultimately have to depend upon except God? Thankfully, He had moved Jack and his sisters to take her in when she had nowhere else to go. At what more pleasant place could she have landed than the Colby Ranch? As for any *inheritance,* the future lay entirely in God's hands, regardless of one's circumstances, but with no past upon which to build, she would have to trust Him completely for any delight that lay in store. The fact that she could, and did, trust Him bathed her fretful soul in peace, at least for a time.

She prayed that Jack could find some measure of that peace, too.

Rolling back the sleeves of his stark-white shirt, Jack glanced into the mirror above his dresser. He needed a haircut, but then he always needed a haircut. Who had time to run into town every few days for a trim? Besides, better shaggy than shorn. Unbidden, an image of Kendra came to mind. She always managed to look polished, even with hardly a thing to her name.

The woman didn't even own a rubber band to keep her hair out of her way. He'd fought the urge to drag her off to a store in town and buy her whatever she needed today. Best not to start down that path, though. Even if she didn't belong to some other man, she wasn't his, and giving her a place to stay while she could figure out her past and future didn't change that. Still, someone had to provide for the woman.

Pushing the thought aside, he picked up the Bible that he'd brought in from the truck after the girls had left for their hen party. He hadn't wanted to say anything, but he'd found the Bible when he'd come by the old Lindley house that evening. He didn't know why he'd stopped there on his way home after treating the cattle. Something had him thinking about the old place and his plans for it, though, so on impulse he'd dropped by. He'd known what he'd found as soon as he'd seen the Bible lying there on the hearth. Both Maddie and Violet had received Bibles with notes tucked inside, but their "mystery gifter" remained just that, a mystery.

He reached over and flipped open the soft, brown, saddle-stitched cover. Inside was a folded sheet of paper. He flattened it out with his palm and read the handwritten words, even though they were the same as those given to his sisters.

I am sorry for what I did to you and your family. I hope you and your siblings, especially your twin, can forgive me as I ask the Lord to forgive me.

Whoever was leaving these notes and Bibles seemed to know a good deal about the family, maybe even more than they knew about themselves. Maddie had received her "gift" back at her place in Fort Worth. Violet had found hers right here. Now this.

Who was this person? And for what did he or she need to be forgiven? He wondered if it could be Brian. That might make sense if Brian was not his and Grayson's father, but then why include Violet and Maddie in the scheme? It just didn't add up.

He'd have to tell his sisters that he had received a Bible and note, too, but tonight hadn't been the right time. Besides, he hated to open up things again. After his mother's accident, he'd vowed not to look for information about the past anymore, but then he'd let Violet and Maddie convince him to do just that—with disastrous results.

He thought of Kendra again. They had more in common than she realized. Oh, he knew his name, but no one could tell him why his parents had split up the family, including two sets of twins! Was Brian Wallace his father? Or was his real father Joe Earl, as Earl's widow, Patty, insisted?

Jack regretted ever agreeing to look for answers in their old neighborhood in Fort Worth. He didn't even remember the place or Patty Earl, the neighbor to whom he and his sisters had spoken. They'd gotten the address because of an old photo that had been restored, and he'd let himself be convinced to go there and nose around, only to come home with more questions and no answers.

The worst of it was that if Joe Earl did turn out to be his father, then his sisters were only his half sisters, and Carter wouldn't even be a stepbrother. Grayson, the twin he'd never met, could be his only full sibling. Jack could just barely conceive of that scenario.

His mother would have been quite young when he and Gray were born, just out of high school, but Jack had a difficult time believing that she would have married one man while pregnant by another. He had a much harder time believing that his sisters could have been fathered by anyone but Belle's husband, Brian Wallace, however. His mother just would not cheat on her husband.

Then again, the woman he knew as Bethany "Belle" Colby was in reality Isabella Wallace. At least he now knew where she'd come by the nickname Belle. He wasn't sure that he wanted to know anything else. Even if Brian Wallace had been around to answer all these questions and not lost somewhere in South Texas—or sneaking around dropping Bibles and cryptic notes in strange places—Jack wasn't sure that he wanted to know the truth, especially not after his mother's accident. Yet, he couldn't seem to think about anything else—except Kendra.

He didn't know which was worse, dwelling on his murky past or the woman without one. At least he knew where he belonged. Come what may, he knew where his home was and would always be, right here on the Colby Ranch. Kendra had no such assurance.

Who was she? Where did she belong? And with whom? Not with him, that was for sure. He couldn't help wondering what was going to become of her, though. She'd come across some tantalizing clues about herself, but what if she never recalled her identity and her past?

And what if she did? She'd almost certainly leave then.

Ignoring the pang in his chest, Jack shoved the note back into the Bible and strode from the room. He needed prayer meeting more than usual tonight. He'd have a great many unspoken requests to go along with the usual prayers for healing for his mother. He'd decide later when he should mention receiving the Bible and note to his sisters.

Looking at the clock on her bedside table, Kendra reflected ruefully that she did, indeed, appear to be an early riser. For the third morning in a row, she had awakened before the sun even rose. She'd dressed then stared out the window into the courtyard below, waiting for Jack to put in an appearance. He hadn't done so, however. That or she'd somehow missed him again as she had on Thursday morning. She wondered if he was avoiding her, surprised by how much the notion hurt.

Lupita had declared today "Pancake Friday," so Kendra didn't waste any more time waiting for Jack. She figured she could get things started. She and Lupita had discussed the menu and cooking techniques the day before, after all.

Hurrying downstairs to the kitchen, she found Lupita and Jack already there.

"¡Buenos días!" Lupita greeted as Kendra entered the room. "The bacon is cooking in the oven."

"What do you mean the bacon is cooking in the oven?" Jack asked, lounging at the breakfast table over a tall mug of coffee. "Since when do you cook bacon in the oven?"

Lupita tossed a glance over one shoulder as she carefully stirred the pancake batter. Kendra went to find salt and vanilla to add to the mix, pausing only momentarily to wonder how she knew to do that, as

Lupita explained, "Since Kendra showed me that it cooks more evenly that way. Takes a little longer, but at least it can all be done in one batch, and the stove doesn't get so dirty."

"Done much cooking, have you?" Jack asked, targeting Kendra with his gaze.

"Apparently," she answered, placing the salt and vanilla extract on the counter.

Lupita lifted her eyebrows. "Yes?" she asked, nodding toward the batter bowl.

"Just a little of each."

Trustingly, Lupita began sprinkling drops of vanilla extract into the batter. Kendra smiled and turned away to test the heavy, cast-iron skillet on a front burner of the stove. She flicked a few drops of water over the oiled surface and watched them sizzle.

"This is ready."

Lupita poured the batter into the pan, making saucer-size cakes that immediately began to bubble up. As soon as the bubbles started to break, Kendra shook back her hair and began flipping the pancakes with a spatula. Suddenly, she felt someone at her back.

"Here," Jack said. Gathering her hair into a clump on the nape of her neck, he quickly twisted a thick, braided elastic band over it, fashioning a ponytail.

Her heart beat at triple speed by the time he finished. "Thank you," she told him breathlessly.

"No problem," he said, tossing a cellophane package of the elastic bands onto the counter beside the stove. “Picked these up yesterday. Thought you could use them.”

She shot a smile at him before poking the package of hair bands into the pocket of her jeans. He had done a very thoughtful thing. Thoughtful and somehow personal.

She tried not to be too pleased. It meant nothing beyond kindness, after all. How could it? No man in his right mind would get involved *personally* with an amnesiac. He couldn’t trust that her past wouldn’t rise up to bite them both.

If that man had also been burned by romance, worried about his comatose mother and confused by the discovery of siblings, including a twin, about whom he’d known nothing… Well, she would be foolish in the extreme to entertain even the thought of a truly *personal* motivation on his part. Likely, he’d just gotten tired of seeing her hair hang in her face.

Still, he’d done a very sweet thing. It proved that he’d been thinking about her. Didn’t it?

She realized suddenly how much she wanted that. It frightened her a little.

She had no right to want such things. She didn’t know who or what lurked in her past. Okay, so maybe she wasn’t a wanted felon. Maybe she wasn’t wanted at all by anyone and for good reason. Maybe she wasn’t such a nice person in her other life, her real life. Surely, that fear lay beneath this sudden need to feel that Jack cared about her personally.

Whatever it was, she would do well to ignore it.

Chapter Seven

Quickly taking a plate from a stack on the counter, Kendra slid a trio of golden-brown pancakes onto it. Lupita elbowed her aside and poured more batter into the skillet before bending to remove the perfectly cooked bacon from the oven.

"Looks good," Jack praised, taking the plate from Kendra and holding it out for Lupita to pile on the bacon.

"Set the fruit on the table," Lupita instructed, nodding toward the refrigerator.

Kendra hurried to comply, taking a bowl of melons and berries from a shelf inside the oversize fridge. She turned to find Jack holding an extra plate. He nodded to the seat to the left of his at the table, where an extra cup of coffee waited. After placing the second plate of pancakes and bacon in front of the cup, he pulled out the chair.

"Sit."

She set the bowl on the table and took the chair

that he'd indicated, nervously wondering what was up, because something surely was. Jack leisurely moved around to his own chair, parked himself and went about slathering butter over his short stack. He poured on the syrup and started to eat. A few moments later, he spoke.

"So what are your plans for the day?" He shot a glance at the housekeeper, adding a wink. "Besides doing Lupita's work."

"I don't do Lupita's work!" Kendra protested. "I just help out where I can."

He stuffed his mouth with dripping pancake then chewed and swallowed before saying, "Shouldn't you be resting?"

"I have a small laceration on my forehead," Kendra reminded him. "What do you want me to do, take to my bed for a week?"

Jack shook his fork at her. "You suffered a hit hard enough to knock your memories right out of your head. I'd say that warrants a few days of rest, at least."

"I'm not ill," Kendra muttered, then switched the subject to ease the tension. "So what are your plans for the day?"

"Gotta wait around here for a feed delivery. Haven't taken care of the stock in the barn yet, so I've got to do that before—"

"I can help," Kendra interrupted.

Jack studied his plate for a minute. "I don't know.

Your health aside, it's not like you're on the payroll, you know."

"But in a way I am," Kendra insisted. "You're paying me in room and board." She touched the ponytail on the back of her head then. "And other things."

"We don't pay our help in rubber bands," Jack grumbled. "We pay honest wages."

"I feel better if I'm contributing," Kendra said, dropping her hand.

Flattening his lips, Jack gave in. "Come along, then. I could use the help. But eat your breakfast first."

Smiling, Kendra began to cut up her pancakes. Jack polished off his and went back to the stove for more, then lingered over a last cup of coffee while Kendra finished eating.

Violet appeared, exclaiming, "Smells good!"

"Does it ever," Maddie agreed, coming into the room right behind her.

Jack grew pensive, running his fingertip around the rim of his cup while his sisters chatted with Lupita and filled their plates.

"Landon's on his way," Violet announced happily, dropping into a chair at the table.

"That's good," Jack muttered.

"Ty and I have a date tomorrow night," Maddie reported, taking a place across from her sister.

Once they both settled in, Jack cleared his throat.

"Need to tell you something."

"What's that?" Violet asked, reaching for the fruit bowl.

"I found a Bible and note at the house."

Both of the twins froze, their gazes locking. Kendra suddenly realized that *the house* was his house, the one he was remodeling.

"When?" Maddie asked quietly.

"Wednesday afternoon."

"And you're just telling us now?"

He made a dismissive gesture with one hand. "It's exactly what each of you found. Well, the Bible's different, but the note's identical."

Feeling the tension mount, Kendra looked from one to the other of the siblings. All appeared grim.

Violet blinked, put down the fruit bowl and stared at her plate. "I wish Mom would wake up," she finally said.

"Me, too," Maddie whispered.

Jack said nothing, but he didn't have to. His expression said it all. Kendra wanted to take his hand in hers, but she didn't really have any place in this discussion. Carefully pushing back her chair, she rose and moved into the kitchen.

"I need to see her right away," Violet suddenly said in a fierce voice. "I need all three of us to see her today. Together."

"I can get there around two o'clock," Maddie volunteered. "The deadlines at the paper are all early today, and I don't have to pick up Darcy until three."

"Count me in as well," Jack said. "I'll just hook up the trailer and pick up the feed at the store, so I won't have to wait around for the delivery guy."

"Then we're agreed," Violet announced. "Two o'clock in Mom's room. Ricardo can cover me for a while."

Jack and Maddie both nodded at their sister.

Having made arrangements with his sisters, Jack motioned at Kendra and led her out into the courtyard and along the path to the barn.

"I'm very sorry about your mom," Kendra told him as they passed through the gate.

He nodded and stopped to pet Nipper as the Australian shepherd loped eagerly toward them. "I just keep praying she'll come around."

"What happened to her?"

"She fell off her horse," Jack answered tersely, dropping to one knee to ruffle the dog's ears. His tone alone let Kendra know that he didn't want to talk about it, and she respected that.

Watching him stroke the dog then lean down to hug it, she wondered about her own mother. Where was she? How was she? *Who* was she?

Even as the questions filtered through her mind, Kendra mentally shied from them. For the first time, she felt a real reluctance to know answers about her past. Reluctance and sadness.

Blocking the feelings, she turned resolutely toward the barn and set off down the path.

Nipper slipped into the barn with Jack. Usually the dog stayed outside, but once in a while he liked to check things inside. Jack had often suspected that the animal sensed when he or others were troubled. Apparently, he wasn't the only one this morning, because Nipper went haring off after Kendra. Maybe the silly old dog just liked the girl. Plenty to like, after all.

Inhaling deeply, Jack left that train of thought as the tranquility of the barn rolled over him. He sometimes complained about having too much to do, but he loved this place and every animal in it. The earthy smell alone could lift his spirits. Something seemed different today, though. A heavy, metallic odor permeated the building.

He glanced around, taking in the loft, the old tractor in its usual spot, the tack bench and the darkened aisle between the pens and stalls. All seemed normal, but Kendra obviously smelled the troubling odor, too.

"That's blood," she said flatly. Then "The foal!"

"Can't be," he told her, following her down the hay-strewn aisle. "Foal's not due for days yet."

Kendra snorted delicately. "That three-hundred-and-forty-day gestation is not written in stone, you know."

Jack shook his head. "I'm not even going to guess how you know that."

She turned once more toward the mare's stall.

Her laughter and suddenly relaxed posture told Jack that they had nothing to worry about.

"Hold the dog," she said, reaching down to turn Nipper's head away from the gate. Jack dug his fingers beneath the dog's collar and held on, though in truth, Nipper showed no tendency to do more than sit and avidly watch. As she carefully entered the stall, Jack hung back with the dog.

"Look at you," Kendra cooed to the wobbly colt struggling up from the bedding, but she made no move to touch the new baby until she had walked around the mare, being careful to keep one hand on the animal at all times.

Only after she'd touched the mama horse with both hands did she approach the colt. Unconcerned, he nosed his mother and began to nurse. Kendra ran her hands over his back, flanks and legs, then felt his neck and mane. The tail of a new foal always looked as if it had been chopped off short, and that never failed to amaze Jack. As if to demonstrate her authority, the mare swished her long, majestic tail over her progeny.

"What are you going to call him?" Kendra asked in a softly modulated tone, patting the colt.

"I'll leave that up to my sister," Jack replied. "The mare's called Roquefort."

"Roquefort?" Kendra exclaimed, glancing in his direction. "That's a funny name."

"The mare was kind of a sickly colt herself," he explained, "and Violet got it into her head that Roquefort Dressing would be good for her. She'd been sneaking out here feeding her bowls of the stuff for days before we found out about it. Violet was just a little girl at the time and had a powerful liking for blue-cheese dressing."

Kendra chuckled and patted the mare's flank. "Doesn't seem to have hurt her any. Maybe we should call him Worcestershire. He's about the right color."

We. A shiver ran through Jack, followed by a pang of regret that this was only temporary. Every day here could be her last. The instant she remembered who she was and where she belonged—to whom she belonged—she'd be out of here. Maybe even before then.

"You and the girls talk it over and decide on something," he muttered roughly.

Nodding, Kendra reached for the leather hackamore that they kept on a fence post, apparently oblivious to the undercurrent. "Let's clean this stall and get the afterbirth smell out of here."

Glad for the distraction, Jack sent the dog out of the barn and closed the door. Then he returned to the stall with a soft rope, which he put on the colt. He half dragged, half coaxed the spunky youngster out into the aisle, while Kendra put the bitless headpiece on the mare and led her out. They snugged the animals together and tethered the mare, then worked for several minutes forking out the filthy bedding and replacing it. Soon the sweet perfume of cedar filled the air, and mother and son could return to their cozy stall.

After feeding and watering the mare, they cared for the other animals. When Kendra remarked that organic feed would be best for the pigs because of how easily they absorbed and retained chemicals, Jack could only stare at her and shake his head.

"I—I seem to have some strong opinions on some things," she apologized, blushing.

"Don't worry about it," he told her with a grin. "Just wish I knew where you came by those opinions." Or did he? Did he really?

"Me, too," she whispered as the cat wandered up and flopped down at her feet. Going to her knees, Kendra immediately began to feel the cat's belly. Suddenly she froze, saying, "I've done this before. I remember distinctly. It was a white Himalayan. She had two kittens. Only one survived."

Aware that she might be remembering something significant, Jack went down on his haunches beside her. "Okay. Just let it come. Now tell me—when and where was that?"

Wincing, she lifted a hand to her forehead. He'd almost forgotten her wound and eyed the almost invisible dressing she'd applied.

"N-not too long ago, I think, but…" Scrunching up her eyes, she shook her head. "I can't remember!"

"It's all right," Jack told her, sliding his arms around her. He couldn't help feeling relieved. She laid her head on his shoulder, and he knew that she fought tears. "It's all right," he said again. "It'll come."

"But what if it doesn't?" she moaned.

"It'll come," he repeated, meaning it as much as a warning to himself as a comfort to her. "Your memories will return. Meanwhile, I think you can take over barn duty, if you want."

She pulled back, gasping lightly. The sparkle in her tear-filled hazel eyes made him want to hug her again. And more. Of their own accord, his gaze dropped to her pretty lips.

"Really?" she squeaked.

Shooting up to his feet, Jack put as much distance between them as he could without being too obvious about it. "S-sure," he said, poking his hands into his rear pockets to keep from reaching down to help her as she rose to her full height. "You obviously know animals, and you've got the routine down. You'll be a big help." The smile that she beamed over him made him want to run, mainly because it made him want to smile, too. "Until you're ready to move on," he added pointedly.

Her smile died by increments, but then she nodded. "I'll take care of the animals every morning before breakfast," she said, "and after dinner."

"That's fine," he said lightly. "Mind you, it's seven days a week now."

"I understand."

"Okay." He couldn't seem to figure out what to do with his hands anymore, so he waved them in a gesture of farewell. "Better get moving. Busy day."

"Thank you, Jack," she told him softly, but he pretended not to hear and hurried away.

He dared not look back or think too hard on what he'd just done—and almost done.

She'd be gone soon, after all. If not before then surely right after her stitches came out. Because what would keep her here then?

Nothing. Nothing at all.

Kendra didn't see Jack at all during the day on Saturday. Violet said that he often stayed out at the old house that he was remodeling and that he'd been unsettled after visiting their mother the day before.

"Why was that?" Kendra asked, curious and more than a little embarrassed about it. "Did anything happen? Do you think she might be waking up?"

Violet shook her head, drawling, "You ought to ask Jack about it yourself."

"Good luck with that," Maddie remarked, walking through the living room on the way to answer the front door. "He didn't exactly want to talk about it when I asked." She sounded hurt by that, but a moment later, she greeted Ty then called out happily, "Don't wait up!"

"Have fun!" Violet called.

Maddie asked where Darcy was.

"Oh, she's with Lupita and Ricardo."

Kendra had learned that Ricardo Ramirez was Lupita's husband and Violet's right hand with the home farm and vegetable stand in town. Kendra didn't say that she could have watched Darcy for the evening. Maybe Ty wouldn't want an amnesiac watching over his little girl. After all, what did anyone know about her?

The two women sat in the family room and watched TV until Landon Derringer came for Violet. He was not at all what Kendra expected. Handsome in an urbane way, he had "big city" stamped all over him, but seeing how Violet rushed eagerly into his arms told Kendra that the two were very much in love. They were kind enough to invite her along on their date, but Kendra declined. The couple had been separated for some time and deserved a bit of privacy.

Kendra tried to watch TV for a while longer, but she couldn't seem to concentrate, so she went upstairs to let down the hem on a skirt that Maddie had given her to wear to church the next day. Curling up on the window seat overlooking the courtyard, she sewed in the hem tape that Lupita had found for her then rose to press the new hem flat. Sewing obviously was not one of her talents, but she supposed the skirt would do. Taking up a book that she'd chosen from the shelves built into one corner of the family room, she returned to the window seat and read for an hour or so before sleep eased over her. Rousing again when she heard Maddie come in, she dressed for bed and slid beneath the covers, falling asleep almost the instant her head hit the pillow.

At some point in the wee hours of the morning, she woke suddenly. Lying quietly, she realized that something had disturbed her—a sound, a movement, something. She got up and pulled on jeans and a T-shirt over her makeshift pajamas. Quietly, she padded out onto the landing in her bare feet then wandered along it around the corner and across the house until she spotted the thin line of light beneath the door to Jack's rooms. Smiling to herself, she went back to her own room and settled into bed again, feeling strangely at peace.

Jack was here. She didn't know why having him near settled her, but she slept soundly for the remainder of the night and went downstairs the next morning in the eager anticipation of seeing him.

He sat at the breakfast table sipping coffee when she came into the kitchen wearing Maddie's altered skirt and a sleeveless sweater suitable for church. She'd even put her hair up, using a pair of elastic bands to capture twists into a kind of bun. The best that she could do for footwear, however, was to ditch the socks that she usually wore with her white leather athletic shoes. Lupita, she noticed, was nowhere to be seen, so Kendra smiled at Jack and offered to get him some breakfast.

"Doughnuts," he said, nodding toward a white, rectangular pasteboard box on the counter. "Lupita keeps them frozen. I usually nuke three or four."

"Or five," Violet quipped, practically dancing into the room. She wore a denim jumper over a pale blue satin blouse and a pair of "barely there" flats.

Chuckling, Kendra carried a plate to the counter and filled it with doughnuts. "Anyone want fruit?"

"I do," Violet said.

Jack just got up and walked out of the room. Kendra sent Violet a questioning glance, but she merely shrugged and went to the refrigerator while Kendra went to the microwave. Seconds later, Kendra set the plate of doughnuts on the table next to the bowl of mixed fruit. Maddie came into the room, looking stylish in a pair of smart slacks and a short matching jacket over a Western-styled shirt. After she poured herself a mug of coffee, the three of them sat around the table eating breakfast and chatting about the previous evening. Maddie and Ty had driven to a neighboring town to see a movie, while Landon and Violet had spent the evening hanging drapes at his newly renovated place, somewhere on the ranch. Kendra hadn't even realized that he *had* a place in Grasslands, though it stood to reason. She didn't see Violet running off to Fort Worth to live.

"Landon has exquisite taste," Maddie observed, waggling her eyebrows at Violet, who blushed.

"He absolutely does," she agreed. "Look who he's engaged to marry."

Maddie laughed. Kendra was still smiling at their banter when Jack returned to the room, carrying a pair of obviously expensive alligator cowboy boots with sharp, metal-tipped toes.

Going straight to Kendra, he crouched and lifted one of her feet to remove her shoe. Standing, he matched the sole of her shoe to the sole of the boot. "Little big," he judged, dumping a pair of heavy socks from the boot into her lap. "I figured as much. Better wear those."

"Uncle James's boots," Violet said with an approving nod. "I should've thought of that." Leaning forward, she said to Kendra, "He was a small man, but he prided himself on his wardrobe."

"I think the boots and a couple of dress hats are all we have left of his things, though," Jack said, walking around the table. "Pity. You might've been able to wear some of his jeans." Sitting down, he began to eat doughnuts.

Touched, Kendra looked down at the shiny, dark brown boots. They would certainly look better with this skirt than her athletic shoes. "Thank you," she said. "I'll take good care of them and return them after church."

"Might as well hang on to them while you're here," Violet said.

"Are you sure? They belonged to your uncle, after all."

"James Crawford wasn't our uncle," Jack stated matter-of-factly. "We just called him that."

"We were the closest thing to family that he had," Violet explained. "Mom came here to work for him as housekeeper. James was pretty old even then. Over time, Mom took over more and more of the ranch for him. When he died, he left it to her. Well, the oldest part of it, anyway. She started adding acreage and included Jack and me in the legal setup."

"I see. That makes the boots extra-special mementos, though."

"They don't do anybody any good sitting in a closet," Jack decreed.

"I'll take extra-good care of them, then," Kendra said, accepting the offer with gratitude.

Violet smiled, and Jack ate his doughnuts while Kendra blinked back silly tears and tried not to read more into Jack's gesture than could possibly be there. They were just borrowed boots, after all.

Borrowed boots, a safe place to stay, elastic hair bands, a shoulder to cry on, a few assigned chores… Every time she turned around, Jack was doing something kind for her. How could she not feel more than simple gratitude for him?

After breakfast, they all trooped out to Jack's truck. As promised, Kendra was wearing Uncle James's shiny boots. Violet and Maddie climbed into the backseat, leaving the front passenger space for Kendra.

The twins chatted all the way into town, leaving Jack and Kendra to ride in silence. At the church, Violet and Maddie immediately paired up with Landon and Ty, leaving Kendra with Jack. He seemed to hang back, sliding into place beside her on the middle pew only at the last moment, as if reluctant to do so. She tried not to be hurt by that. It wasn't as if they were a couple, after all, and he had been more than kind. She had no reason for complaint.

Fixing her full attention on the service, she soon discovered that behind the horn-rimmed glasses of the red-haired, freckle-faced minister, Jeb Miller, stood a capable man of God. The good reverend couldn't have been more than thirty and tended to teach more than preach, but he quoted lengthy passages of Scripture with the ease usually provided by a teleprompter and spoke with simple but unassailable wisdom. She noticed, too, that retiring little Sadie Johnson, with whom Kendra had chatted at the First Wednesday meeting, sat virtually enraptured at the front of the church during the sermon.

Afterward, Jack practically sprinted for the back of the church, leaving Kendra to shuffle along with everyone else who crowded the central aisle. A tiny, elderly woman at Kendra's side squinted up at her through the thick lenses of oversize eyeglasses, asking, "Do I know you?"

Kendra's heart lurched. "I'm not sure. Do you?"

The woman tapped her chin with a gnarled finger, tilting back her head to stare at Kendra through her bifocals. "You look familiar."

"Were you at the First Wednesday gathering?"

The old woman shook her head. "Don't get out much in the evenings at my age."

"Have you seen me somewhere else?" Kendra asked hopefully.

Surely, if she'd been to Grasslands before, someone would have recognized her by now. Still, it could be that she hadn't been around in some time—or that she was related to someone who lived around here, someone who looked a lot like her. An unreasonable hope rose in her, painful in its intensity. She felt total recall hovering somewhere in the back of her mind, as if one little jolt would open the floodgate of memories for her.

"No," the old dear said, narrowing her eyes. "I think it was here at the church. I just can't remember when."

"Can you try to recall?" Kendra heard herself ask, wincing at how pathetic she sounded. She clamped her jaws shut and mentally prayed instead.

Please, Lord. I have to know who I am and where I belong.

She held her breath, waiting to see what God would do in that moment.

Chapter Eight

The old woman stared at her, unaware that Kendra's whole life hung in the balance.

"I can't be certain," the elderly lady said, smoothing her thin, silver hair, her delicate, knobby hands sweeping from her wrinkled brow to the lopsided bun at the nape of her slender neck. "Seems like it was a long time ago, though."

Kendra felt her bottom lip tremble and clamped down on it with her teeth. "I—I'd appreciate it if you could remember," she encouraged gently.

After staring at her for several seconds longer, the feeble woman offered a sweet smile. "I'm Bessie Lindley," she said. "My late husband Albert and I used to ranch a small acreage that's part of the Colby spread now."

Kendra managed a wan smile. Not wanting to give her adopted name or explain her situation, she said, "I'm a guest there."

"Ah," the woman commented, "maybe I have

seen you around town, then." Mrs. Lindley shook her head. "That's old age for you. Something that happened years ago you remember clear as a bell. What happened yesterday, pfft!" She tilted her head in an oddly birdlike gesture, chirping, "You do look familiar, though."

Kendra's heart pounded with fresh hope. Somehow, Jack overheard the conversation and made his way to Kendra's side, moving against the tide of the crowd.

"Miss Bessie," he said, inclining his head. "Hope you're keeping well."

"As well as old age permits, Jack," she replied, lifting a hand to pat his cheek. "I was just telling this young lady here that she reminds me of someone."

Jack shifted so that his shoulder touched Kendra's and sent her a meaningful glance. "Any idea who that might be, ma'am?"

Bessie Lindley shook her head. "Most likely, it would be someone from long ago." She chuckled, adding, "Can't remember what I had for breakfast, but something that happened fifty years ago… Well, it couldn't be important."

Kendra swallowed a lump in her throat. If only Bessie Lindley knew! Jack lifted a comforting hand to the small of Kendra's back.

Mrs. Lindley squinted up at Jack and asked, "How are you coming with the house?"

While Jack gave a rundown on the improvements

that he'd made with the Lindley's former home, Kendra tried not to let her disappointment reduce her to tears. Presently, she felt Jack apply pressure to her back. He ushered her up the aisle, past the pastor—who briefly shook their hands—and out of the building.

"Let it go," he whispered as he walked her across the graveled drive to the greensward beyond. "Just let it go."

"Do you think it means anything?" Kendra asked, effectively ignoring his advice. "Maybe I was headed here, after all. Maybe I have f-family or…" She broke off, trying desperately to convince herself.

He steered her to a bench placed beneath a mature pin oak and all but pushed her down onto it. "Could be," he answered, parking his hands at his waist. "Or perhaps simply you remind Bessie of someone else—someone completely unrelated to you. She's an old woman. She said it herself. She can't remember what she had for breakfast."

A tear fell from Kendra's eye and rolled down her cheek. She quickly wiped it away. "It's just…" She saw the pity in those light brown eyes and gulped. "N-not belonging anywhere or to anyone, it's like not e-existing, like I'm not even real." She wiped furiously at the tears that now streaked her face.

Twisting about, Jack sank down onto the bench next to her and looped an arm about her shoulders. "I never met anyone more real than you," he told her, "and you do have a place in this world. For as long as you need or want it."

She tried to smile but mostly managed a sniff. "Thank you. The thing is, though, I sense that I've felt this way my whole life, as if I don't quite belong or fit in."

"Aw, come on," Jack said, giving her a quick squeeze. "A woman like you could fit in almost anywhere. You fit in with the Colbys well enough. Better than some I could mention," he muttered.

"If you mean Maddie, that's not fair," Kendra told him softly.

Jack looked at her with some surprise. "I didn't mean her, but what makes you think I did?"

"You seem to have a hard time equating her with Violet," Kendra ventured quietly, glad to have something else upon which to focus.

"Haven't known her as long as I've known Violet," Jack grumbled.

"It's not just Maddie, though, is it? It's your brothers, too."

Dark brows drawing together, Jack stared at her. "What do you know about my brothers?"

"Mainly what I've overheard," she admitted.

Jack shook his head. "Leaving Carter out of it," he began quietly, "I just keep asking myself what reason a mother could have for splitting up her family of two sets of twins and hiding them from one another. Especially if Brian is not my and Grayson's father. Talk about a messed-up situation."

"All I know," Kendra told him earnestly, "is that I'd give almost anything to discover that I have siblings, whatever the circumstances. And to find a twin… How wonderful that would be!"

"I'm not so sure of that," Jack mumbled, squinting off into the distance. "Sometimes the price for such a thing is just too high."

Kendra couldn't resist the impulse to lay a hand upon his knee. "I don't understand. What do you mean?"

Jack looked down at her hand. Just as she was about to take it away, he covered it with his own larger, stronger one. He didn't move again as he told her in a low voice how he'd badgered his mother for information about their past and family, how they'd argued and she'd jumped onto her horse that day and ridden away at breakneck speed.

"I'll never forget how she looked," he said woodenly, "crumpled there with her head bent beneath her."

"Her neck is actually broken?" Kendra asked, horrified.

"No," Jack said, shaking his head. "If—*when*—she wakes up, she ought to have full movement. Mouse didn't even step on her that I could tell."

"Mouse," Kendra echoed. "That would be the grulla mare in the barn?"

"Yes."

She understood now. "That's why you warned me to stay away from the horse. You're worried that the same thing could happen again." Kendra found that deeply touching.

"I can't have another tragedy like that on my conscience," he said, frowning.

Surely he didn't think that the accident was his fault or the horse's. "No one is to blame," she said.

Shaking his head, he looked up and sucked in a deep breath. "I wish that were true," he muttered just before getting to his feet and walking away.

Kendra watched him with an aching heart. She couldn't help hoping that a deeper feeling than misplaced guilt rooted his concern for her, but what right did she have to any emotion from Jack? She couldn't forget that she might be engaged to some other man. It seemed unimaginable, but how could she know?

"Here you go, Lupita," Jack said, handing her the pale blue envelope on his way to the lunch table on Monday.

"Thank you," Lupita replied sliding the envelope into the pocket of her apron.

Just as soon as Belle woke up, Jack had decided to speak to her about setting up an automatic debit system with their bank. That alone would save hours of work every two weeks. Meanwhile, he'd do things as his mom had done them, printing and signing checks and distributing them throughout the day. Only one envelope contained cash. Surprised to see Maddie at the lunch table, he placed the blue envelope as nonchalantly as he could beside Kendra's lunch plate. He'd meant what he'd told her the day before: so far as he was concerned, she had a permanent place at the Colby Ranch. To his mind, that meant she was now on the payroll.

Kendra looked at the blue envelope. "What's this?"

Rather than answer, Jack let her open the envelope and take out the money. It wasn't much, just a few hours' pay for the help she'd given him and Lupita.

"But you only gave me the job of feeding the animals a couple days ago," she said, eyes shining.

He shrugged, sat down and picked up the sandwich that Lupita had put in front of him. Maddie, who also sat at the table, cleared her throat. Jack ignored her and bit off a huge chunk of sandwich.

Smiling, Kendra asked, "Is anyone going into town this afternoon? I really need to pick up a few things."

Jack looked pointedly at Maddie, expecting her to volunteer. Obviously, she wasn't working at the newspaper today. His sister shook her head.

"Sorry. I got a text from Grayson earlier. He's finished his undercover assignment and has been catching up on everything that's happened with the family. We're due for a long phone conversation. That's why I took the afternoon off from work."

Jack pulled in a deep breath to try to keep from asking, "Does he know about me, then?"

"You and Violet," Maddie replied gently. "That's one of the reasons we have to talk."

Jack didn't know how he felt about that. More to the point, how did Grayson feel about having a twin? Pushing aside the thought, he glanced at Kendra, who stood there watching him with a mixture of hopefulness and expectation. He just didn't have the heart to disappoint her.

Swallowing, Jack wiped his mouth with a paper napkin and said, "I have to pick up some materials myself. You can ride in with me after lunch."

Maddie and Lupita shared a conspiratorial glance, but Kendra, thankfully, seemed too excited to notice. She hopped up off her chair, saying that she would run and get ready. Jack couldn't imagine what she had to do. She couldn't look any better than she did now. He shook his head and realized that both Maddie and Lupita were grinning at him.

"Don't you two have anything productive to do?" he grumbled, frowning at his sandwich.

"You're the one with time to run into town in the middle of a workday," Maddie observed innocently.

Jack scowled. Biting her lip, Maddie hastily rose and hurried from the room, while Lupita chuckled and clucked her tongue.

Of course, both Lupita and Maddie were aware of his attraction to Kendra. Probably everyone who saw him and Kendra together was aware of it. Sadly, that didn't make the attraction wise. He mentally ticked off the reasons.

First and foremost, even without a ring, Kendra could very well be engaged—or even married—to another man. Even if she wasn't, however, some man somewhere was bound to be waiting for her return. That irked Jack more than he wanted to admit, but it only stood to reason. A woman like her attracted men like honey attracted flies. If his own life wasn't so complicated at the moment…

He shook his head. Complicated barely covered the mess that was his life, which brought him to the second unfortunate reason why he had no business getting personally involved with Kendra or any other woman. He still had no idea how this family stuff would eventually shake out. He didn't even know what last name he could claim in the end. The timing couldn't have been worse.

Besides, once his mother woke up, he'd have everything he needed, and he'd do well to remember that fact. If he'd taken that attitude earlier, his mother wouldn't be lying comatose in a hospital bed, but instead he'd badgered her for information.

With shock piled on top of shock and mystery on top of mystery, he really didn't need Kendra pushing him to accept Maddie, Grayson and Carter into his life. So why, he wondered as he polished off his lunch, did the memory of her impassioned words on the subject foster the tiniest bit of guilt in him? He frowned, pondering that, but then she appeared with her pants legs stuffed into the tops of James's old boots and one of Violet's shirts tied at her waist, her wavy, pale gold hair brushed to a lustrous sheen, and he forgot the question.

Had he thought her lovely? No. She was beautiful, breathtakingly beautiful. And he was in trouble. He gulped and shot to his feet, obeying the urge to run.

"Ready to go?" she asked brightly.

"Uh." Seeking to justify the abruptness of his actions, he nodded. "Best get moving. Lots to do."

"Okay," she said, blinking as he stepped out from behind the table and strode off at a near run. She followed along behind him, her footsteps tapping rapidly across the floor.

He grabbed his hat on the way out the door and crammed it onto his head. Why on earth, he asked himself, had he offered to take her to town?

But he knew why, and his impulse to help her, take care of her, *please* her, scared him. After all, he did not have room in his life for any woman, especially one with her kind of trouble.

On the way to town, she chattered happily about being able to buy some new things and how much she enjoyed taking care of the animals, but when he didn't comment, she eventually fell silent. As they pulled into the parking lot of the ranch supply store, she nervously asked where he was going to be while she shopped. Realizing that she needed to purchase some personal items, he told her that he'd be in the back picking up building supplies that he'd ordered previously. Promising not to be long, she bailed out of the truck and went inside.

A little over thirty minutes later, she showed up with two large shopping bags in tow and a mile-wide smile.

"That was fast," Jack declared. He'd expected to be waiting for an hour at least.

"They're having a sale," she announced happily. "I'm practically broke again, but at least I have more than one set of clothes now."

"Good deal," Jack said, finding her smile infectious. He took the bags and stowed them in the backseat while two men loaded the last of several prehung doors.

"Where do these go?" she asked, running a hand over the bare wood.

Jack found himself reluctant to tell Kendra what he intended to do with these doors. He didn't want to remind her of the disappointment she'd suffered at Mrs. Lindley's hands after church on Sunday. However, Kendra put it together without him having to say a thing.

"Oh, these must be for the house you're remodeling," she surmised, her hazel eyes sparkling. "Bessie Lindley's old place."

"That's right."

"I got the impression that Mrs. Lindley is glad to see the house restored," Kendra remarked.

Jack had to smile. "She seems to be."

"I know the house is on the ranch," Kendra mused, "but I'm sure it's not part of the main compound."

"No, it's out off Franken Road," he told her carefully.

She didn't seem to recognize the name. Smiling, she said, "I'd love to see it."

On impulse, he decided, "I'll show you where it is. I need to drop off this load, anyway."

Kendra beamed at him. "Great!"

He signed the receipt while she climbed into the truck. She was buckled in by the time he slid behind the wheel. On the drive out of town, she asked what had induced him to start remodeling the old house.

He shrugged. "I don't know. I just always liked the place. Plus, I admired Bessie's late husband, Al. He was a real fine cattleman and a good friend of James's. It always seemed sad to me that the Lindleys never had any children so they didn't have anyone to pass the place on to. Al's father built the house over seventy years ago. Doesn't seem right to just let it sit and rot away."

"It's a great thing you're doing. I like the idea of an old house being brought back to life," Kendra said.

"You haven't seen it yet," Jack reminded her, but he couldn't help being pleased with her attitude.

He intentionally chose a route that took them up Blackberry Hill. As they drew near the curve at the bottom of the steep incline where she'd wrecked her car, Jack waited for her to recognize the area, but she seemed oblivious. They were coming from the opposite direction than she had that day, though. He said nothing, just drove the truck around the curve and up the hill. Another mile or so farther on, he turned into the rocky drive.

"How far now?" Kendra asked.

"Just over this rise," he told her. They bounced over the rutted drive and down into the yard.

The two-story house sat in a little valley between two enormous pecan trees. Wrapped on three sides by a deep porch and flanked by lilac bushes, the old stone structure made a homey picture.

"Oh, how pretty!" Kendra exclaimed.

Pleased, Jack grinned as he brought the truck to a halt. "I like it. I'm thinking of putting on a metal roof."

"Yes. Definitely." Indicating a pile of stone nearby, she asked, "Did you do the masonry work?"

"Not on the outside. That's original. I did the fireplace inside, though, and I've been gathering stone to build a garage. Thought I'd come off this end here with it." He pointed toward the back corner of the house. "That door there leads right into the kitchen."

"I like that idea," Kendra told him, preparing to exit the truck.

He got out and met her at the front bumper, saying, "I'm planning on cutting a circular drive here."

"That's good," she enthused. "Maybe you'll have enough stone left over from the garage to line it."

"Hadn't thought of that," he admitted. "That would look good."

He led her up onto the porch and pulled out his house keys. He'd started locking up after he'd found the Bible and note here on the hearth.

She looked around, saying, "It would be nice to have a couple of rockers out here. Maybe a swing."

"I want a swing in that tree there," he said, pointing. "I mean, if I was a kid, I'd want a swing there."

She laughed and preceded him into the large living room. The staircase stood just inside the door, and she ran a hand over a spindle that he'd spent an hour sanding.

"Stain or paint?" she asked.

"Haven't decided yet."

"Stain, definitely," she said, nodding. She crossed the floor to take a closer look at the massive stone fireplace. "Just imagine sitting here on a cold winter night."

"I have," Jack admitted, "many a time."

They went on to inspect the dining room, kitchen, laundry room and the downstairs bedroom and bath, the latter of which he had added, along with a sizable closet. He was surprised that she advocated a wood floor even for the kitchen, but she agreed that tile would be best in the entry area.

They went upstairs even though it was basically

an open shell with only the bathroom fixtures set and stacks of lumber everywhere.

"I figure two bedrooms up here," Jack said, "in order to have ample closet space."

"Are you going to finish the attic?" she asked, looking up.

"Guess I could," he mused. "That'd give us another bedroom."

Her gaze collided with his. "Us?"

"Me," he corrected, glancing away.

She stared at the ceiling. "It could be a sewing room, or a playroom or just storage."

"I don't sew," he said around a grin.

"I don't think I do, either," she admitted with a chuckle. "Still, it's a great house."

"You sound ready to move in," he observed quietly.

"Oh, I would," she replied dreamily, "if it were mine. And finished."

He cleared his throat. "Well, it's not ever going to be as fine as the big house…."

"That doesn't matter," Kendra said without missing a beat. "This will make a wonderful home, and it has history on its side. I see what you mean about the Lindleys. This is a house that just cries out for children." Looking around her, she added wistfully, "I hope I have a place like this waiting for me somewhere."

That made Jack frown. He didn't like to think

of anything waiting for her that wasn't right here. "Maybe you do."

She shook her head, looking stricken. "I can't imagine it, really. When I try to, I feel…bleak."

"What will you do if you find that you're engaged to marry a man you can't remember?" Jack heard himself ask.

"Don't even say that," she begged, reaching up to press her fingers against his lips. She dropped her hand again instantly. "I don't believe it, but if it should turn out to be true, I can't see how I could go through with the wedding. I couldn't be in love with someone else and feel this way about—"

She didn't complete that thought. She didn't have to. Even as Jack told himself that she couldn't really be falling for him, some part of him rejoiced. Before he knew what he was doing, he had lifted his hands to her upper arms and pulled her to him. What could he do then but kiss her?

As her lips yielded to his, she slid her arms around his neck. He angled his head, using the brim of his hat to shield them and create a little cocoon of intimacy, a world with just two people in it. He felt like Adam to her Eve, as if he had just received the gift of the one woman created just for him. For all he knew, Eve could be her name.

A more sober thought followed that whimsical one. She could be anyone—anyone but the woman for him. If such a person even existed, she couldn't be this one. Not now, not given all the mysteries and problems plaguing both of them.

Lifting his head, he stepped back and let his hands fall.

"I'm sorry," they both said in unison.

"That shouldn't have happened," he ground out.

At the same time, she said, "That wasn't wise."

"If my life was just less complicated," he offered huskily.

"If I knew who I am…" she began, shaking her head.

They stared at each other, neither happy about the situation, until he muttered, "I need to unload the truck."

She nodded and swept her hands over her arms as if suddenly chilled. He felt rather cold himself, and it had nothing to do with the temperature, which hovered at almost ninety degrees.

Without another word, he turned and went down the stairs. She finally came down while he was lugging the next-to-last door into the living room. Immediately taking hold of one end, she helped him stack the door and its frame atop the others then traipsed out to the truck behind him and helped him haul out the last one. Afterward, he locked up, while she settled into the truck cab.

The way back to the main house did not involve Blackberry Hill. Jack couldn't help being glad about that. She needed to remember everything that she could, but he knew that she'd likely leave as soon as she did. Resuming her old life was probably for the best—even if it didn't feel that way now.

Chapter Nine

Kendra curled up in the window seat and looked out over the softly lit courtyard, feeling glum. It couldn't be denied—Jack was avoiding her. He hadn't been at breakfast, lunch or dinner for two days in a row, and tonight he hadn't even come to the midweek prayer service. Maddie had seemed as stricken by that as Kendra felt. She'd overheard the twins whispering about it, with Violet insisting that Maddie was not the reason for Jack's absence. Kendra had resisted the impulse to blurt that Jack was avoiding *her,* not Maddie, but then she'd have to explain about that kiss, which she couldn't explain even to herself. Besides, she suspected that Jack did use every excuse to avoid Maddie. So far as Kendra could tell, she'd actually had more interaction with Jack than Maddie had. No doubt, he would be the same way with his twin, Grayson.

Kendra couldn't help feeling that would be a mistake. She didn't understand the whole situation, of course, and it was obviously very complicated, but not to embrace family, whatever the circumstances, seemed tragic to her. What she wouldn't give to discover that she had a twin—or family of any sort.

She couldn't help feeling a bit sorry for herself. Drawing up her legs, she bowed her head until her brow rested atop her knees. She hardly felt the wound on her forehead and had only reapplied the flesh-colored bandage earlier this evening so the people at church tonight wouldn't be troubled by her injury, but that didn't make her feel any better. If only her memory would heal as quickly as this minor laceration. Closing her eyes, she went straight to God.

I know I should be thanking You, Lord, and I do. I could have been out on the street with nowhere to go and nothing, not even a name. But You brought me here to the Colby Ranch and these kind people. I know I belong somewhere else. Help me regain my memory so I can figure out where that is....

Pausing, she bit her lip. Truthfully, she hated to think about leaving the Colby Ranch and Grasslands. Tonight at church, she'd felt almost as if she'd belonged here. Everyone had been so concerned for her. Even Bessie Lindley had been there. Having realized Kendra's predicament, the old dear had wanted to come, she'd said, to apologize for making so much of finding Kendra's face familiar. Kendra had urged her to think nothing of it and then had tried to put Mrs. Lindley at ease by talking about the improvements that Jack was making to the former Lindley house. When she'd been there on Monday with Jack, Kendra had felt as if she'd come home, especially when they'd kissed.

No matter how ill-advised that kiss had been, it had felt like balm to her soul and made her feel wanted and treasured, as she so desperately needed just now. But once she remembered her past, she would have to go. Anticipating the pain of that, she almost wished that God had spared her this time at the Colby Ranch. Surely, He had a reason for it all, though, and she felt that she had an inkling as to what that might be.

A knock at her bedroom door startled her. To her surprise, she found Jack there when she opened the door.

Without preamble, he said, "Doc Garth's office called."

"Oh?"

He nodded. "They suggested we come in first thing in the morning to get those stitches out. That work for you?"

"Of course. I'll get the barn stock fed early."

"No hurry," Jack told her lightly, one corner of his lips crooking up. "First thing in the morning for Doc is nine o'clock."

Kendra smiled. "He should spend a few days on the ranch."

Jack chuckled. "Naw. We need Doc doing what he does."

"True."

He started to turn away, and Kendra found herself stepping forward to stop him. He lifted a brow in obvious question.

"Speaking of doing, you must've been busy the past couple days."

He looked away, nodding, and shifted halfway around as if eager to be gone.

"I suppose you have a lot to do," she went on lamely.

He paused but said nothing. She wished he would open up to her. Instead, he seemed determined to push her away. Well, she wasn't going to make it easy for him.

Thinking quickly, she stepped through the door and pulled it closed behind her, saying, "I think I'll just head down and find a cool drink. Care to join me?"

Jack slid a look at the stairs. Then, as if he'd reached a decision, he visibly relaxed. "There's some lemonade in the fridge."

"That sounds good," Kendra told him, smiling.

He gave his head a little jerk as if to say, "Follow me." So she did.

"I guess you got those doors hung," she ventured carefully as they descended the stairs.

He nodded. "Yep."

"That's good."

They walked on in silence until they entered the kitchen. Kendra looked through the breakfast room window at the softly glowing courtyard beyond. “It looks like a nice night outside. Think I’ll have my lemonade on the patio,” she said, hoping he’d join her.

He shot her a quick glance before going to the cabinet to take down a pair of tall glass tumblers. At the same time, she went to the refrigerator for the lemonade. They came together again a moment later over the island. She picked up the tumblers and turned to the refrigerator, filling them with ice via a dispenser in the door.

When she placed the glasses on the island again, Jack poured the lemonade then handed one of the drinks to her. Sipping carefully, she went to the door of the breakfast nook, pleased when he followed. Choosing a pair of chairs with a small table between them, she sat down in one. Jack took the other chair, and for several minutes, they drank in silence. If he wasn’t quite engaging with her, Kendra thought, letting the cool liquid slide down her throat, at least he wasn’t avoiding her any longer.

Suddenly, Jack spoke. “I know you don’t understand my attitude toward Maddie, Grayson and Carter.”

Kendra closed her eyes in silent thanks that he had broached the subject that so troubled her. Leaning forward, she said, “It’s just that, given my own situation, I can't imagine not welcoming a previously unknown sister or brother."

"I get that," Jack replied softly, staring at his drink. "The thing is… Maddie and Violet might be my sisters, in which case Carter wouldn't be any relation to me at all."

Now, that surprised Kendra. She understood suddenly that Jack was trying to protect himself from too much emotional attachment. Obviously, he didn't want to be hurt if the truth somehow limited his connections to Maddie and Carter, but what about his twin?

"That means Grayson," Jack went on, as if reading her mind, "could be my only full sibling, but what if he doesn't—" Breaking off, he cleared his throat before saying quickly, "I don't even know him! Twins are supposed to feel some *connection,* but what I mostly feel is shock. Does that make sense?"

"Absolutely," Kendra murmured. "To suddenly discover that you have siblings you never knew about is one thing, but to discover that you have a twin… That has to be disorienting."

"Disorienting?" Jack echoed with a snort. "More like overwhelming. With Mom in a coma, all these secrets coming to light, Maddie on the scene, and both she and Violet suddenly engaged to marry, I'm just not sure this is the time to bring someone else into the mix."

"But aren't you at least curious about Grayson?" Kendra asked.

"Of course! When I think of him, though," Jack admitted bleakly, "I can't help thinking that he grew up with the father I've always wanted."

"Oh, Jack." Her heart broke for him.

"If Brian even *is* our father," Jack plowed on. "There's a woman in Fort Worth who swears that her dead husband fathered me and Grayson. She believes my mother was already pregnant with us when she married Brian and that Mom chose him because he would be the better provider or something."

"That's..." Kendra shook her head, astounded. "I don't know what to say."

"There's nothing to say," Jack muttered. Then abruptly he growled, "The only two people who could say anything factual about it aren't talking. Mom's sick, and Brian's..." Jack threw up a hand. "Nobody knows where Brian is. That's the problem!"

Kendra puffed out a deep sigh. "Jack, I'm so sorry. But surely you see that Grayson is in the same position as you. He grew up not knowing his mother."

"Yes, he did," Jack insisted. "He had a father *and* a mother. Until she died."

Kendra wrinkled her brow, trying to put that information into perspective. "But that would have meant... She had to be his stepmother."

"So? At least he had someone," Jack grumbled. "*They* had someone. Maddie didn't even know that the woman wasn't their real mother until she and Violet stumbled across each other in Fort Worth a couple months ago."

"I take it that Carter is this other woman's child," Kendra surmised, her mind whirling.

"Yes. Hers and Brian's."

"Which means that if Brian isn't your father, then Carter isn't any relation to you at all."

"You got it."

"Still, at the very least, Maddie is your half sister and Grayson is your *twin*," Kendra argued. "If he's as like you as Maddie is Violet—"

"I don't know what he is!" Jack snapped. "We've never even met."

"Why not?" Kendra wanted to know. If Jack was the problem, she intended to argue vociferously that he meet with his brother.

"According to Maddie," Jack muttered, "he's been undercover but should be surfacing soon."

"Undercover?"

"He's a cop and was on some top-secret assignment or something."

Kendra briefly closed her eyes, relieved to discern that Jack hadn't purposefully kept his brother away.

"What about Carter? Have you met him?"

"No. He's in the military overseas. I think he'll be stateside in November, maybe."

Kendra lifted her eyebrows. Their chosen professions said volumes about the Wallace/Colby boys. She felt a moment's intense relief that Jack hadn't felt the need to take such risks as Grayson and Carter. She supposed that, being the man of the house, the responsibility that he'd had for his mother and sister had kept him closer to home.

"I'll pray for their safe return," Kendra told him softly.

Jack nodded, replying softly, "Thanks. Maddie says they can handle themselves, but you can't help worrying. Just have to leave it in God's hands, I guess."

That told her much more than he probably intended. For one thing, he obviously felt concern for both Grayson and Carter. For another, he'd been praying for them himself.

"You're a good man, Jack," she declared impulsively.

His gaze darted to hers, his dark brows drawn together almost comically. "Why do you say that?"

"If you weren't a kind, caring, responsible Christian man," she answered, "you wouldn't have taken me in after the wreck."

He mumbled something about his sisters.

"Your sisters have been very welcoming," she stated firmly, "but they weren't the ones who brought me here. You did that. I hate to think where I'd be if you hadn't. Thank you."

Shaking his head, he muttered, "You don't have to thank me."

"I know," she admitted. "I also know that Maddie wants to be your sister in just the same way that Violet is. It doesn't matter whose father was who, Jack. It only matters that Maddie cares. And that you do, too."

He didn't let his gaze touch hers, but a smile tugged at his lips. "For a girl who doesn't remember her own name, you sure know a lot," he grumbled.

Kendra chuckled. "What I know," she said, "is that you and the Lord will work it out in time."

He met her gaze then, admitting, "It helps to talk things out with you."

She couldn't quell a spurt of joy. "Why?"

"It's not just that you're unbiased," he began, shrugging. She only wished that she was unbiased, but she wouldn't argue the point. "You're…clear," he went on, "about what's most important, I mean."

"When you have no past, you have nothing on which to base a future," she pointed out. "That means you have only the present. And yes, some things do seem starkly clear to me. For instance, nothing matters quite so much as having someone to care about you and somewhere to belong."

To her surprise, he reached out and caught her hand in his. "You have those things. This is your home for as long as you need it, and no matter who else out there is a part of your life, we are, too, now." Squeezing her fingers, he settled back with his lemonade. "I like to think that we're, well, family. Of a sort."

Smiling, Kendra returned the pressure, clasping his hand tightly. They weren't real family, but somehow, he had become her lifeline.

"I thought you were avoiding me," she confessed.

"I was," he admitted. "Can't avoid the truth, though."

"What truth is that?" she asked warily.

"That neither of us is in a position to start a romance, but both of us can use a friend."

Thank You, Lord. This truth, though, pricked at her heart.

"That sounds about right to me," she said in a soft voice.

He nodded. "Friends it is, then."

"Friends," she affirmed. After a few moments, she said, "As a friend, can I ask you something?"

"What's that?"

"Will you tell me about your mom?"

Jack chuckled. "She's a firebrand. She went to work for James Crawford when I was a little boy, and after his death she turned his gift into the biggest, finest ranch in northwest Texas." He looked around, saying proudly, "She built this house, did the very best that she could by me and Violet." Frowning, he added, "If I'd had a father, I'd have to say that my life had been as near to perfect as it's possible to be."

"That doesn't sound like a woman who would

willingly leave a daughter and son behind," Kendra mused.

"You're right," Jack agreed solemnly. "That's what doesn't make sense. She's a loving, hardworking Christian woman who never shirked a responsibility that I could see." He shook his head. "I just don't get it."

"There has to be a good reason," Kendra said, clasping his hand. "Hold on to that."

Smiling introspectively, Jack nodded. "I'll try. Meanwhile, maybe you'd like to see her? Tomorrow, after the doc takes out your stitches, I'd planned to stop by the nursing home with Violet and Maddie. You're welcome to come, too."

"I'd like that," Kendra told him.

They sat in silence after that, holding hands and listening to the ice shift and clink in their glasses.

Everything had changed, Kendra realized, and yet nothing had changed. She still didn't know who she was or where she belonged, but in this moment she felt utterly content. Clasping Jack's hand, she didn't have to wonder why.

"Meet you at the convalescent home," Violet said through the window of her idling SUV.

"As soon as the doc is finished with Kendra," Jack confirmed.

Violet nodded, glanced knowingly at Maddie, who sat on the passenger side of her vehicle, and drove toward the convalescent home next door to the clinic. Jack sighed inwardly. Those knowing glances were less perceptive than either of his sisters assumed. Yes, he felt a keen attraction and a certain responsibility to Kendra. But so what?

Neither he nor Kendra could get involved in a romance now. They had agreed that anything more than friendship was simply out of the question. Even if they hadn't come to that mutual realization, he'd have to be nuts to fall for someone who couldn't remember her past. What if she suddenly remembered that she was wildly in love with some other man?

Shaking his head, he stepped up onto the sidewalk next to Kendra.

"Something wrong?"

He offered her a lame smile as he walked toward the building. "Nope. Just don't want you to be late for your doctor's appointment."

"We should be fine," she told him, passing through the door that he held open for her.

Inside, Doc's receptionist had them sit in the empty waiting room. Two more folks came in right after them. A third, fourth and fifth appeared before the nurse came for Kendra. She rose and started forward, only to pause and glance back at him.

"You coming?"

Jack warred with himself for a moment then rose to follow her. Nurse Hamm parked them in a treatment room and took Kendra's vitals before disappearing again. Mere moments later, Doc Garth walked in. He slit the seal on a heavy plastic envelope containing tiny scissors and tweezers while shooting questions at Kendra.

"Any headaches?"

"No. Just some tenderness."

"Blackouts?"

"No."

"Dizziness?"

"None."

"Strange dreams or memories?"

She told him about feeling that she'd been in the backseat of the car when it wrecked.

"Well, that didn't happen," the doctor drawled as he began to snip and tug loose the stitches on her forehead.

"I know," Kendra conceded, "but that's what flashed through my mind when I saw the car."

"Did you go out to the site of the accident?" Doc asked, continuing to work.

"No."

"Yes," Jack corrected, glancing at Kendra. "We drove out that way a few days ago."

"We did?" she asked in a small voice.

Nodding, Jack said, "She didn't seem to recognize the spot, but we did approach it from the opposite direction."

Kendra bit her lip, tears filling her eyes. Doc finished extracting the stitches, blotted a couple specks of blood with a gauze pad and instructed Kendra to keep the scar covered with sunscreen.

"Do that, and it should disappear entirely."

"All right," she agreed softly. "What about my memory?"

Doc Garth sighed and peeled off his gloves. "It's anybody's guess. I can't tell you when, or even *if,* your memory will return."

Ducking her head, Kendra dashed tears from her eyes. "I see." She sniffed and lifted her head. "I've got a problem, then, don't I? What am I going to do now?" It turned into a wail at the end, and she clapped a hand over her mouth.

"We've already settled this," Jack said matter-of-factly, taking her by the arm. He tugged, helping her down off the examination table. "You're going to the nursing home with me, then you're going home to the ranch," he went on, "and this evening you're going to feed the animals again because that's your job. Okay?"

Smiling through her tears, she vigorously nodded her head. They left a few moments later. When her hand stole into his, Jack clasped it tightly, aware of twin bubbles that rose in his chest, one of delight, one of regret.

"I don't understand," Jack said testily. "Is she coming out of it or not?"

"No one knows," Violet told him, glancing toward the narrow hospital bed where their mother lay quietly, as if asleep.

"But the nurse did say that she's been mumbling

from time to time and pulling at her tracheotomy tube," Maddie supplied.

Jack turned back to the bed, afraid to hope. Belle had never so much as stirred during one of his many visits. She had seemed to sigh once or twice, but he couldn't even be sure about that. A movement at the side of the bed caught his eye, but it wasn't Belle moving; it was Kendra. She brushed the back of Belle's hand with her fingertips and bowed her head. He knew that she prayed for his mother's recovery and mentally added his plea to hers.

Please, Lord, let her wake up soon. Let her wake up and be her old self.

Aware of a whispered discussion going on behind him, he turned to frown at his sisters. They stood together in the corner of the small utilitarian room and stared back, twin expressions of bland unconcern on their faces. He knew that look. Lifting his hands, he flexed his fingers in the international sign for "give."

"What aren't you telling me?"

"It's not Mom," Violet said quickly. "It's Brian."

Jack's frown deepened. "What about him?"

"I'm very worried about Dad," Maddie confessed. "I got an email from Grayson this morning. Now that he's finished his undercover assignment, he's made some phone calls, and he's been told that Dad might be ill."

"You mean, that may be why Brian's dropped out of sight?" Jack clarified.

"That's what Gray thinks," Maddie confirmed. "Oh, how I wish Grayson could just go down there to investigate!"

"What's the holdup?" Jack asked, stung more than he wanted to admit that Maddie seemed to automatically discount him as being of any help in the matter. Well, if he and Grayson were twins, they ought to be equally capable, right? Besides, hadn't he been with her and Violet in Fort Worth when they scoped out Belle and Brian's old neighborhood?

"Debriefing," she explained. "He has to get all the right information to all the right people, submit a bunch of reports, that sort of thing. Once he's fully debriefed, he'll be free to leave, but it's all complicated by the fact that he's injured. Could be weeks before he can get away."

Jack frowned. "How serious is his injury?"

"A dislocated shoulder," Maddie said. "He says it's nothing, but it's obviously slowing him down."

"Did you tell him that I got one of those Bibles and mysterious notes?"

"I told him," Maddie confirmed, "but I just don't get how it's all connected."

"We don't know that it is," Jack pointed out. "The Bibles and notes might not have anything at all to do with why Mom and Brian split the family or with Brian's disappearance, but someone obviously knows more about us than we do. I mean, whoever it is knows exactly where to leave those things for us to find, but we don't even know what this person did or when."

"Grayson is as puzzled as we are," Maddie said, "but maybe he can figure out the mystery."

"Our parents would know," Violet put in, looking toward the bed. "They have to."

"Which is one of the reasons why I think I should go to South Texas and look into things," Jack stated flatly, irked that he'd had to volunteer and more disturbed than he wanted to be by Grayson's injury and Brian's possible illness.

"I think that's an excellent idea," Kendra interjected, appearing at his elbow. "You could drive down to where Brian was last seen and talk to the people there."

"Yeah," he said, buoyed somewhat by her unwavering support. "I could do that. Maddie and Ty made the trip last month and found Brian's cell phone. This time, I could speak to the pastor of the church himself and try to figure out where Brian was last seen and why they think he might be ill."

"It's a long drive to manage alone," Maddie pointed out with studied nonchalance. It had exactly the result he figured she'd intended when Kendra volunteered to go with him.

"I can't drive, but surely I can be of some use."

"Oh, I'm sure you can," Violet assured her.

Jack rolled his eyes as Violet and Maddie exchanged one of those "twin" looks again. He felt sure that he and Grayson would never do that, not if he and Gray were truly alike. If they did happen to be carbon copies of each other, then Grayson would be just as independent and opinionated as Jack himself. They sure wouldn't be walking in lockstep, let alone playing matchmaker in the most obvious ways. No, sir. He couldn't help wondering what his sisters were thinking. Didn't they realize that neither he nor Kendra were in a position to entertain romantic notions? Still, he appreciated Kendra's support and welcomed her company for what promised to be a chancy task.

"I'll give you the telephone numbers of my contacts in the area," Maddie offered. "I'm sure we can arrange accommodations for the two of you with them."

"That'll be fine," Jack replied tersely. "I'll see what arrangements I can make tonight, then." He looked to Kendra. "Maybe we could leave in the morning."

"Works for me," Kendra said, smiling.

He looked to Maddie then, saying, "And *you* can take over for Kendra in the barn." That would teach her to meddle.

Maddie's mouth dropped open, but then she clamped it shut again and nodded, while Violet hid a grin behind her hand, saying, "Sounds like a plan."

Glancing at his mother's still, silent form, Jack hoped it proved to be a plan that could provide them with at least some answers, because he very much feared that they wouldn't get to the bottom of it any other way.

Chapter Ten

Yawning, Jack sat forward behind the steering wheel and pressed his shoulders back and together, stretching as best he could within the confines of the truck. Kendra reached for the thermos of coffee that she had filled before they'd left the house that morning. After showing Maddie what to do in the barn, she and Jack had enjoyed a hearty breakfast then set out in his truck. Kendra poured coffee into the tall, metal cylinder of his travel mug and screwed the top in place before opening the drinking spout.

"Thanks," Jack said, flopping his head from side to side as he reached for the mug. He took a long drink of the still-warm brew.

"The least I can do is pour your coffee," Kendra said.

With no license to show, she dared not get behind the wheel, even if Jack had trusted her to drive—and she couldn't blame him if he didn't.

She'd wrecked a car before, after all, and lost her memory in the accident.

"Just the company is help enough," Jack told her.

She hoped that was true. Last night, while they'd been planning this trip, she'd felt confident that they were doing the right thing. Yet later, alone in her bed, she'd begun to worry. What if they discovered that Brian had died? What if they found Brian and he confirmed that he was not Jack and Grayson's father? What if they found no trace of Brian?

As if reading her thoughts, Jack suddenly said, "The more I think about it, the more I'm afraid that Brian is dead."

Kendra closed her eyes. "It is possible."

"But at least we'd know, right?"

"Well, yes," she agreed hesitantly. "Knowing is better than not knowing, I suppose."

"Yeah, that's what I think, too," Jack said. He shifted in his seat then, admitting, "The thing is, I really don't want him to be dead."

"Of course you don't."

"In fact, I—I'm starting to hope that he is my father. You know?" He shot her a glance fraught with uncertainty. "At least then I'd have a chance to get to know my dad. I mean, no matter what the story is, no matter why he and Mom split up the family, I'd have a chance to know him."

"That's what I've been praying for," she told Jack.

"Maddie says he's a good guy." A muscle ticked

in his jaw as he stared ahead at the long stretch of road. "She pretty much thinks he hung the moon."

"Oh, I don't think so," Kendra disputed. "She loves him, and she admires him. I mean, he's a doctor who volunteers his services to treat the less fortunate, so he's smart and dedicated and caring. But I hear some discontent in her voice when she speaks of their relationship."

"I've heard her say that he wasn't always there for her when she needed him," Jack murmured, "but that he wanted to be."

"Maybe he wanted to be there for you, too, but couldn't," Kendra suggested gently.

Jack said nothing for a long while, then, "I'd like to think so."

Me, too. Oh, me, too. She wanted Jack to have a father's love. She wanted that for him even more than she wanted to regain her memories, and if she'd stopped to think about that for even a moment, she'd have known just how much trouble she was in.

They stopped for lunch and dinner, which made for a twelve-hour day. By the time the truck pulled into the small community of Blackstone, Kendra felt a bone-deep fatigue that she knew Jack shared. In fact, because he had driven the whole way, exhaustion probably rode Jack harder than it did her.

Thanks to the truck's GPS system, they were able to drive straight to the parsonage of Pastor Patrick Sanchez. A small, slender man in his early sixties with thinning gray hair and a pencil-thin, salt-and-pepper mustache, Pastor Sanchez did not look Hispanic, despite his surname. They spent about an hour with him, listening to him praise Brian and the work he had done in the area.

"Unfortunately," said Pastor Pat, as he preferred to be called, "the last word I had of Brian, he was at a migrant camp in the area, but he apparently left sometime in the night. I'm told that he seemed ill, feverish and weak."

Jack looked at Kendra, and she knew that the same thoughts that troubled her also troubled him. Why had Brian left so precipitously? Had he been too ill to know what he was doing?

"You are both tired," the pastor said kindly. "Let us pray, then I will show you to your accommodations."

Jack would be staying with the pastor, but Kendra would be the guest of an elderly widow, who lived across town. Jack and the pastor drove Kendra to Mrs. Osequia's small, modest home, where the pastor introduced them. Thanking the plump, friendly widow, Jack pressed Kendra's hand and took himself off to a much-needed bed at the parsonage.

Kendra gratefully sank into a hot bath in an ancient, claw-foot tub. Afterward, she practically fell into the clean, narrow bed in the tiny room to which she was shown. On some level, she was aware of the open window and lazily circling ceiling fan, but she fell asleep before the thought registered that

Mrs. Osequia lived in deep South Texas without the seemingly necessary benefit of air-conditioning.

The sun blazed by the time they found the migrant camp the next morning. Kendra sensed Jack's impatience as they searched for those who were known to have last seen Brian Wallace. Once they at last located the camp, Kendra's Spanish came in handy.

It was just as Pastor Pat Sanchez had reported, however. Brian had arrived at the migrant camp on Monday of that week. By the end of the day, he'd appeared feverish, flushed and weak with a slight cough and rusty voice. He had assured his patients that his condition was not communicable, but many remarked that he had seemed sicker than those he had come to treat. He had declined to share the evening meal with those in the camp, saying only that he wanted a quiet place to rest until his ride came. No one could tell Kendra who had brought Brian to the camp. He had been dropped off by someone unknown to those there. Apparently, he had been picked up well after dark by the same person or someone else. Either way, no one knew who had provided his transportation.

Frustrated, Jack took out a map and, using his truck's GPS, plotted out all the hospitals and clinics within a two-hour drive of Blackstone. Armed with a plain paper photo printed out by Maddie, they set out to see what they could discover. More than once they were told that privacy laws precluded medical personnel from giving out any information about patients, but in almost every instance, they were at least able to ascertain that Dr. Brian Wallace had not received treatment in the area. It helped that Brian was known to many in the local medical field, and that the two hospitals and half a dozen clinics were small and relatively informal. Nevertheless, Jack and Kendra returned to Blackstone that night discouraged and no closer to locating Brian Wallace than when they'd started.

Dispirited, Jack grumbled that Grayson could probably have found some sort of lead.

"In any event, we won't give up," Kendra assured him.

To her surprise, Jack lashed out. "I'm not sure I even want to know the truth anymore."

"Yes, you do," she refuted gently. "You're just disappointed."

"We've hit a brick wall!"

"Not necessarily," she argued. "We might still find some answers in Fort Worth."

Jack collapsed back into his seat, sighing. "I can't think of that right now."

"I know you're worried," she told him softly. "So am I, but at least we can pray knowledgeably for Brian now."

Jack nodded. "That's true. I just hate to disappoint Maddie."

Kendra smiled fondly. "Your sister will be grateful that you've tried to find your dad," she assured him.

"Do you really think he is my father?" Jack asked softly, his brown eyes beseeching her.

Kendra pondered that for a minute, then she nodded. "Yes, I do. I don't know why, but I do."

A smile tugged at the corners of Jack's mouth, but worry quickly turned them down again. "Thanks for your help," he told her. "I'll pick you up in time for church tomorrow morning."

Leaning over, she kissed his cheek, feeling his prickly five o'clock shadow against her lips. He leaned his head against hers for a moment, but he did not turn his face and kiss her as she foolishly wished he would, which was undoubtedly for the best. And sadly disappointing.

During worship that next morning, Pastor Sanchez mentioned Brian and requested prayer on his behalf. That necessitated quite a lot of handshaking, murmured thanks and terse explanation after the service, so the hour had progressed well past noon by the time Kendra and Jack were able to climb into the truck and head back to Grasslands. They disappointed Mrs. Osequia by declining her invitation to lunch but with such a long drive ahead of them, they dared not delay. Instead, they picked up burgers and ate in the truck along the way.

Kendra did her best to make conversation. Jack had called his sisters the evening before to give them the bad news that they now knew conclusively Brian was ill but were no closer to actually finding him. Kendra tried to assure Jack that none of this was his fault, but as the day wore on and the miles and hours ground away, Jack brooded more and more. Kendra sensed his withdrawal and the turmoil behind it, but she couldn't seem to lift him out of his doldrums. She resorted to silent prayer, and somewhere between midnight and 2:00 a.m., she dropped off to sleep.

Jack woke her by gently pushing her hair out of her face. "This is getting to be a habit," he said wryly, standing in the doorway of the open passenger door.

"Huh?" Straightening in her seat, she blinked sleep from her eyes and inhaled sharply. A moment later, she registered the fact that they had arrived at the ranch house. Apparently, Jack had parked, gotten out and come around to her side to wake her.

"At least you're aware this time," Jack said, reaching across her to release her safety belt. "And not wearing a veil."

Twisting sleepily to dangle her legs out the door, she muttered, "Yeah, there is that."

Placing his hands at her waist, he pulled her out of the truck. Her arms naturally slid about his neck, but as soon as he set her feet on the ground, he stepped back, breaking the contact. He moved quickly to haul her suitcase out of the backseat. Maddie had loaned Kendra a small overnight bag for the trip, and Jack set it on its rollers, pulling up the handle.

Kendra stepped forward to take the handle, but Jack refused to relinquish it, muttering, "I'll get it."

Too tired to argue, Kendra led the way into the house. Someone had left a light on for them. They trudged through the house to the staircase nearest the kitchen and began the climb, Jack carrying her bag. At the landing, he finally yielded it, whispering, "G'night."

"Jack," Kendra whispered, "I'm sorry we didn't find Brian."

Sighing, Jack nodded. "Me, too."

"Please don't give up," she urged him.

"Maybe that's what God wants me to do," he retorted. "Maybe I should have given up on my past a long, long time ago. If I had, maybe Mom would be here now and Brian would be…doing whatever it is that he does."

"You didn't cause your mother's accident," Kendra told him, "and you certainly didn't cause Brian's illness. And whatever the reasons behind the split up of your family, that's not your fault, either."

He studied her for long, weighty moments with sad eyes before his lips curved in a smile. "You're good for me," he said, then he leaned in and lightly kissed her cheek, whispering, "I'm sorry."

She didn't know why he felt the need to apologize, but she realized as he went back down the stairs that he hadn't brought in his own bag. Far from resolving the issues that kept Jack from fully embracing his new-found family, the trip that she'd so heartily endorsed had, instead, driven him even farther away from those who loved him.

"I am sick and tired of excuses!" Jack snapped, glaring at Ty. The tall, lanky cowboy had ridden over to the Lindley place to inform Jack that the last alfalfa cut would have to be delayed by at least another twenty-four hours.

The laconic ranch foreman propped an elbow on the horn of his saddle and pinched his chin between the thumb and forefinger of his hand, calmly drawling, "If the old baler breaks down, the old baler breaks down, Jack. A fact is a fact."

Jack ground his teeth, knowing that Ty was right, but they were pushing the calendar already and the last alfalfa cut yielded the sweetest grass and smallest hay bales. The big bales that they got from the summer cuts could be left out on the range under tarpaulins to preserve their quality until they were needed for winter forage, but the small bales went into the barn for use there. Unfortunately, they still depended on Uncle James's fifty-year-old baler for the small bales, and when it broke down these days, replacement parts usually had to be handmade. That played havoc with the harvest schedule, which was tricky, at best.

"So what do you want to do?" Ty asked. "Wait another day or leave the last field as is to fallow?"

Jack sighed, weighing the issues before making

a decision. "Cut it." They needed every bale they could grow to get them through the winter. Ty muttered agreement and wheeled his mount. At the last minute, Jack called out to him, "Hey, Ty."

The cowboy set the horse back on its heels and looked over one shoulder. "Yeah?"

"Sorry I barked at you. I'm in a foul mood."

Ty grinned in that slow way of his. "Uh-huh. Haymaking does that to a fellow." He touched his heels to the flanks of his horse and rode off, chuckling.

Jack scowled and stomped back into the house. Haymaking, as if that was all he had to concern him. Ty knew otherwise. No doubt, he was privy to all the family secrets now, thanks to Maddie. What Ty couldn't know, though, was how desperately Jack wanted Brian to be his father. He wanted the man to turn up safe and sound and be glad of having another son. While he was at it, he wanted his mother to wake up and be her old self again. He wanted to know the truth about his family and why they'd split up.

And he wanted Kendra.

Stupid as it was, he'd gone and let himself fall for her. Knowing that she wasn't free to return his feelings, that she would surely be leaving them as soon as her memory returned or someone from her past tracked her down, Jack had still let his heart become entangled. He didn't even know her name, let alone where she might be from, but that didn't matter. In her presence, he felt hopeful, whole. He wanted her to be the woman he believed her to be. He wanted her to be free. He wanted more than her gratitude and friendship.

He wanted any number of things that he couldn't have, and staying away these past three days hadn't done a bit of good. If anything, staying away had made the wanting keener. He'd prayed, and he'd contemplated, and he'd worked until he fell into an exhausted slumber each night, and still he had to wonder what God could be doing.

Why would God allow his family to be split? What purpose could Belle's coma possibly serve? How could Brian get lost while serving God? And why bring a beautiful amnesiac into the mix? None of it made sense. To his human way of seeing things, none of it offered anything to the situation except more angst.

Sighing, Jack looked around him. He'd started hanging gypsum board upstairs, but he hadn't done much down here. He ran a hand over the newel post, remembering that Kendra had expressed a preference for stain over paint. Then he wondered if he could ever live here without thinking of her, without wanting that for which he dared not wish.

Bowing his head, he decided that he would not attend prayer meeting again that night. Given his surly mood, he and everyone else would be better off if his prayers were accompanied by the pounding of nails.

As in the days before, he worked late into the night. He did not, however, think he could settle down to sleep at the house tonight. Strangely, he felt a need to be at the big house at the main compound that night. He wanted a real bed and a hot shower. He wanted to feel others around him even if they were all asleep.

Slipping into the darkened house around midnight, he expected everyone—especially Kendra, a notorious early riser—to be fast asleep. He hadn't taken four steps along the upstairs landing, however, before he realized that someone waited outside his door. As soon as she rose from the chair that she'd placed there, he knew who it was. He couldn't help a thrill of delight, even as he sought to avoid her.

"It's late, and I'm tired."

"I'm tired, too," she said, folding her arms. "I'm tired of you avoiding me."

He started to deny that he'd done any such thing, but honesty compelled him to mutter, "It's just my way of dealing with things. I have to step back to get some perspective sometimes."

She made a delicate, snorting sound. "Great. Then you surely realize that you can't avoid the issues of your past forever."

Mimicking her stance by folding his arms, Jack

put his back to the wall. "Look, I went to South Texas, didn't I?"

"Yes, and when that didn't turn out as you wanted, you came right back here to hide from your problems."

"I wish," he muttered.

"To *try* to hide from them, then."

When she was right, she was right. "Point taken."

"All right, then," she said, "so what are you going to do about it?"

"What *can* I do?" he asked sourly.

She stated the obvious. "You can get yourself to Fort Worth and ask some questions. I've asked some questions myself, and I know that you have the address of the house where your family lived when you were small. You can go door-to-door, if you have to. Someone has to remember your family and—"

"We've done that," Jack interrupted, "and we came away with more questions than we started with!"

"So? At least you have a place to start. That's precious, Jack. I don't think you can realize how precious. You can't understand what I would give for any clue, any hint of just a place to begin asking questions about my past."

He exhaled, sharply. "And what if I don't find answers this time?"

"Then you won't be any worse off, will you?" she retorted. "But you won't know unless you go."

Well, he couldn't argue with that, and he resented the fact because he could already feel the hope rising in him.

"God had to put an amnesiac in my way," he muttered.

"Maybe that's the only way He could convince you to do something this important," she said.

"This stupid, you mean."

"It's not stupid to seek the truth," she said firmly, "and if my amnesia is the price for you finding out the truth about your past, then it's worth it to me."

The utter selflessness of that statement both humbled and thrilled him.

"Oh, Kendra," Jack said, reaching out to cup her cheek with one palm, her long golden hair tumbling across his arm. "You delight me and break my heart all at the same time."

She said nothing to that, merely bowed her head.

He pulled her into his arms, just holding her. His cheek resting against the top of her head, he let himself feel whole and comforted for several long moments, until she whispered against his chest, "Want some company on your trip?"

Jack chuckled. "Don't think we'll be needing your Spanish this time, but sure."

She sighed with contentment and his arms instinctively tightened around her.

"We'll head out Saturday morning," he decided. "That'll give us time to rest up and make our plans."

She pushed away then, saying happily, "Maddie and Darcy are going to feed the animals."

Jack shook his head, laughing softly. "I should have known you'd have it well in hand."

"I just want to help," she told him.

"Sure you do," he said. "I may not know much about you, but I know that."

"Don't feel bad," she joked wryly, skipping away, "I don't know much about me, either."

Chuckling, he watched her go. Actually, he reflected silently, he knew quite a lot about her. He knew that she was a treasure, no matter what her name might be. She didn't have a lazy bone in her body, yet she possessed a peacefulness that he felt even amidst all the turmoil of his own life. She was bright and beautiful, kind and thoughtful, caring and brave, quiet but not timid, gentle but not weak. God knew that she had certainly accepted her circumstances with far more grace than he had accepted his, and despite being lost, and confused, her thoughts were more for others—for him—than herself.

What he didn't know was how a woman with no name and no past could be everything that he had ever wanted.

Chapter Eleven

Knowing that Jack was in the house and resolved to keep digging into his past, Kendra slept well. As usual, she woke early, despite staying up late the night before, and hurried out to the barn to find that the heifer had delivered a healthy calf but was in some distress. She thought about examining the heifer, momentarily struck by the fact that she knew exactly how to go about it. Instead, she rushed back to the house. Relieved to find Jack at the breakfast table, she blurted out her concerns.

"You need a vet to take a look at the heifer. She's delivered a calf, which seems just fine, but something's not right with the mama."

Jack's dark brows drew together as he took out his cell phone. When he got the veterinarian on the line, he said simply that he had a late-springing heifer in need of treatment.

"Not sure," he said in reply to something that the

other person obviously asked. "Haven't seen the cow myself. I'll let you talk to the one who has."

He offered the phone to Kendra. Uncertain, she gingerly took the small rectangle and lifted it to her ear. "H-hello?"

"Yeah," said a sleepy, male voice, "what makes you think there's a problem?"

The words tumbled out of Kendra's mouth without thought. "The calf is several hours old, but there's no afterbirth. The heifer is agitated but not straining."

The animal doc sighed. "Okay. Be there as quick as I can. Tell Colby to have a thermos of coffee ready. I had a late night, and I'll need it."

"It'll be ready," Kendra promised. The vet ended the call, so Kendra handed the phone back to Jack, who calmly pulled his plate forward and began to eat again.

"Shouldn't we get down to the barn?" she asked.

Jack shrugged. "Can we do anything?"

She thought about it and shook her head. "Not really."

"Well, then, we'd better eat while we can. It'll take Dr. Anderson a while to get here. He's got to come from Plainview."

"Plainview? Where's that?"

"About fifty minutes southwest," Jack answered.

"That's awful!" Kendra exclaimed.

"Yep. We make do on our own as often as we can, but sometimes we just have to wait for the vet."

"Maybe we could get the calf to nurse," she said, thinking. "That might help start new contractions."

"Okay," Jack told her approvingly, "but first we eat."

Lupita sat a plate of sausage and eggs in front of her, but Kendra shook her head. "I'll just make another pot of coffee first. The doctor said to have a thermos ready when he got here."

Jack chuckled. "Tom always wants a thermos of coffee ready, even in the middle of the afternoon in July." He nodded at Lupita, saying, "We know what to do. Relax."

Kendra sat down and made herself eat, but she couldn't help thinking about that heifer. The moment that Jack pushed away his empty plate, she popped up to her feet. He rolled his eyes. "Let me get my hat."

She followed him into the hallway and out through the carport to the truck, which he drove down to the barn, explaining, "I find that when Doc Anderson is around, I'm often sent to town for one thing or another. Might as well have transportation on hand."

He parked the truck next to the corral on one end of the barn and got out. Kendra hurried around the truck to slip through the metal-pipe fencing. The heifer ignored her, but the calf bawled and trotted around behind its mother. When it tried to nurse, the heifer sidestepped. Jack went to the toolbox in the back of the truck and took out a length of rope while Kendra ran her hands over the heifer in an effort to soothe it before slipping around to catch the calf in her arms. It kicked, but she managed to immobilize and calm it. As she approached the heifer with the calf, Jack lifted a loop, twirled it and neatly tossed it over the heifer's head, drawing her in and snugging her to the corral fence.

"Whoa there, mama," he crooned. "We don't mean any harm."

Kendra carried the calf to the mother and went down on her haunches, pressing its nose to the udder. The cow sidled away. Kendra followed with the calf, effectively trapping the skittish cow against the fence. This time, when she pressed the calf's nose to the udder, it quickly latched on to a teat, so Kendra let it go and rose, backing up a step. The heifer bawled a protest, but didn't kick the calf away. Dr. Anderson pulled up more than half an hour later and gave the heifer an injection. Within minutes, the heifer delivered a second, stillborn calf then dumped the afterbirth.

Beside herself with regret, Kendra knelt beside the dead calf, murmuring, "I should've thought of that, checked for a second heartbeat."

"Wouldn't have found one," the older, heavyset man decreed, groaning as he got down on one knee next to the lifeless body. "Look at the misshapen nostrils."

Realizing that the calf had never been viable,

Kendra whispered a Latin term, *"Sinus clauditur nares deformis."*

"You know something about animal medicine," the veterinarian stated, jowls quivering. "Wouldn't be looking for work, would you?"

Kendra stared at him with wide, agonized eyes. Was this something she could consider? How did she know what she knew? And even if he would hire her without a real identity, how could she leave Jack? The weight of it all suddenly felt immense, and she quite unexpectedly burst into tears.

She heard boots hit the ground as Jack leaped over the fence. Then he gathered her into his arms and pulled her to her feet.

"Hush, babe. You're not responsible for this."

"I know, but—"

"You did all you could, more than anyone else could."

"It's not that," she sniffed.

"We've got one healthy calf, and that's all we ever expected," he pointed out.

That was something, at least, Kendra told herself. Nodding, she swiped at the tears that trickled down her cheeks. "You're right."

"I want you to go to the house," Jack said. "You're tired, and you need to rest. Take the truck. I'll walk or ride back with Tom."

"I'll walk," she insisted, embarrassed by her outburst. "I walk twice a day. It's not far, and it'll do me good."

Jack smoothed her hair and cupped her face in his hands, his golden-brown eyes holding hers until he leaned forward slightly and placed a gentle kiss in the center of her forehead. Smiling wanly, Kendra pulled away. She needed to be alone, to think, to pray. To remember. Yet, remembering could take her away from the one person she most wanted to be near.

She shut off that train of thought and numbly crawled through the fence to walk around the corner of the building, intending to cut through the barn and out the front. The dog, Nipper, ran up to her, tail wagging and tongue hanging out of its mouth. Pausing, she stooped to pet the animal, instinctively knowing that doing so would lift her spirits. She heard Tom Anderson say, "That's quite a gal you've got there."

She lifted her head, listening for Jack's reply. "Yes, she is," he said. "Quite a woman."

"New romance brewing?" the affable veterinarian asked offhandedly.

Kendra's heart stopped beating until finally Jack answered with a dull, "No."

She closed her eyes against the tears that welled once more. Then she sucked in a deep, tremulous breath, ruffled the dog's fur, then went on her way, determined not to be disappointed. What else could Jack have said, after all? What man in his right mind would romance a woman who didn't even know her own name? What man found the woman of his dreams in a wrecked car, wearing a bridal veil with her blue jeans?

She wished suddenly that she had not volunteered to accompany him to Fort Worth tomorrow. But what choice did she have? He needed to open himself to his past so he wouldn't close himself to his family, and she needed to know that he would be well after she had gone from here. For surely she must go. Soon.

After the events of the morning, Jack couldn't bring himself to stay away from the house. He needed to be near Kendra in case she remembered, in case she…needed him. To keep busy, he updated the books. It was all done by computer now, from cattle registration to tracking expenses, but that didn't make it any less time-consuming, especially as Belle had kept up James's habit of making entries in a daily diary, noting the activities on the ranch. Jack scribbled notes here and there and tried to keep up, but he really had no heart for recordkeeping. He resorted to dumping in comments about the work he'd done on the Lindley place, and a visceral yearning unexpectedly took hold of him.

He seemed to need to be wherever Kendra was, even though being near her had become as much pain as pleasure. He couldn't forget that every moment could be his last with her. She could remember in a flash all that she'd left behind—and then leave *him* behind. That being the case, tomorrow would be both torture and treasure, but he couldn't bring himself to forego the latter in order to avoid the former.

Kendra seemed even more quiet than usual at lunch and dinner, not even speaking when, at the evening meal, he informed his sisters that he and Kendra would be traveling to Fort Worth the next morning to see if they could dig up any more clues about the family history.

"Oh, I'm so glad!" Maddie said. "Do you want me to see if Gray can meet you there?"

"No," Jack said automatically, noticing the way that Kendra frowned.

"He might be able to get away, and I'm sure he could help," Maddie pressed.

Jack made himself relax and smile appreciatively. "I'm sure he could, but I don't want anything to delay Grayson getting to South Texas to look for Brian."

Maddie subsided immediately. "Right. Good thinking."

"Finding Brian is more important than answering questions about the past," Violet agreed.

Kendra said nothing, just pushed her chuck-wagon beans around on her plate. Jack let the subject drop, only to find himself bringing it up later when they happened across each other on the patio late that evening.

She sat on the ground, legs folded, petting Nipper. The foolish thing instantly abandoned her to trot over to Jack. He spent a few seconds ruffling the dog's mottled gray, black and brown fur, while Kendra got to her feet.

"I know you're upset with me," he began, before she could move away.

She shook her head. "No. Not upset. I'm more… concerned."

"What I said to Maddie is true," Jack insisted. "Finding Brian is more important right now than getting answers about the past."

"But is that really why you don't want Grayson to meet us in Fort Worth?" Kendra asked gently.

Jack clamped his jaws, but those hazel eyes could see the truth. Sometimes he thought they saw straight into his heart.

Finally, he shook his head. "I'm just not ready to meet my twin. I…I don't know how to have a brother. All I've ever had are sisters."

"Sisters," Kendra echoed, emphasizing the plural.

A smile played around the corners of her lips, and the fact that he was so pleased to see it made him grumble, "I mean, *a* sister."

"Uh-huh. Because you don't really think of Maddie as your sister."

He barely, mostly, controlled a grimace. "I'm… starting to."

Kendra's smile widened. Then she laid a hand lightly in the center of his chest. "I just don't want to leave here thinking that you're at odds with the rest of your family."

"Leave?" He seized her by the upper arms. "Have you remembered something?"

"No," she answered quickly. "I haven't remembered. But surely someday I will regain my memories."

Jack relaxed, relief sweeping through him. "Maybe not," he said, sounding more hopeful than he'd meant to sound. "You heard what Doc Garth said. Your memory might never come back."

Dropping her gaze, she swallowed hard. "That's true, but I've been thinking about the car."

"What about it?" Jack asked, frowning down at her.

"It's a really nice car," she said, "and it didn't just materialize out of thin air. Someone within the mileage on the odometer has to be looking for it, and when they find it—because they *will* find it, if only because the police put out inquiries using the vehicle ID number—then they'll find me, and that has to lead...somewhere. Don't you think?"

He hadn't thought at all, Jack realized. He'd only brooded. Now that she had brought up the subject of the car, though, he could see that she was right, and the thought horrified him. The only surprise was that someone hadn't come for the car—and her—already! It had been nearly three weeks since he'd seen that hot red car driving too fast along Franken Road. Why hadn't someone connected with the car, if not the veil, come looking for her? He would have, and he'd only known her for three weeks.

Three weeks?

How had she come to mean so much to him in only a few weeks?

She looked down at his hand, which gripped her arm too tightly, as if he could *make* her stay with him. Releasing her, he abruptly stepped back.

"Better get some sleep," he muttered. "We need to be out of here by 5:00 a.m."

She nodded, smiling wanly. "Right. That's early even for me."

"Good night, then," he said, but she was the one who turned away, only to pause after a single step and look back at him.

"I'm sorry about the second calf, but thank you for not doubting me this morning, about the heifer, I mean."

Jack blinked at her. "Never crossed my mind to doubt you."

Nodding, she told him, "Your confidence in me means a lot. Thank you."

He didn't know what to say to that, so he said nothing at all. It truly had not occurred to him to doubt her. She obviously had a gift when it came to animals and a great deal of knowledge, even if she didn't know how she'd come by it.

"Tom said you did just right by putting the calf to nurse," he told her.

She smiled at that before giving the dog a last pat and going into the house.

The alarm went off at 4:15 a.m. Kendra jerked awake, one thought in her head.

Fort Worth with Jack.

She took a moment to ask God for a successful trip then jumped into the shower. Afterward, she threw on her customary jeans and a simply tailored, Western-style blouse of lime-green cotton printed with raspberry-pink flowers. Uncle James's boots tempted her, but her athletic shoes were the more sensible choice. She put together a little bag of things to take with her: a tube of lip gloss, a comb, an elastic band, a package of breath mints and the few dollars that she possessed.

Having no identification had proved surprisingly freeing. She didn't have to worry about carrying around a driver's license, credit card, insurance information or anything of that sort. Having no name also meant that she had no Social Security number, however, which meant that her income couldn't be reported. She realized that if she worked for long, her employer could get in trouble, which made her wonder how she would survive until her memory returned.

Kendra refused to think that her memory would not return, even though at times, she almost hoped that it would not. Whatever waited in her past could be less than spectacular, after all. The circumstances of her accident seemed to indicate that she had been running away from something—or someone—and remembering whoever or whatever that was could result in her leaving Jack and the ranch. Even if she did not return to her old life, however, that didn't mean she could stay here. Whatever she'd blocked out could very well turn Jack and his family against her, but even if that were not the case, she would not subject them to more difficulty. They already had enough of that. So her memory must return, and she must go. But not today, thankfully.

Today was for Jack and Fort Worth.

Once again, they climbed into the truck with a full thermos of coffee and a well-programmed GPS system. Jack seemed in an upbeat mood, and Kendra made up her mind to enjoy every moment with him.

"I'm glad we're doing this," she admitted softly.

"Me, too," he said. "I have the feeling that things could be different this time. I mean, something's gotta go my way sometime, doesn't it?"

"Oh, Jack," Kendra chided, "how can you say that? I understand that you've had some nasty shocks and you're worried about your mom and Brian, but I hope you can see how blessed you are."

"That's true," Jack agreed. "One of the best things that ever happened to us was being taken on by James Crawford. We called him Uncle James, but he treated my mother like his daughter and Violet and me like grandchildren."

Kendra smiled softly. "It must have been wonderful to have had that kind of relationship with him.

"The thing is, though," Jack admitted, "my relationship with James just made me miss my father and real grandparents more. I couldn't help wondering about them and wishing…" He shook his head. "We've had a good life on the ranch, but…" He took a deep breath and plunged on, "I have to ask myself why Grayson was the one Brian chose to keep and not me. I know that's foolish and immature, but—"

"We don't know what happened. You don't know that Brian chose Grayson and Maddie over you and Violet any more than you know that your mother chose you and Violet over Grayson and Maddie. I mean, can you see your mother doing such a thing?"

"No," Jack replied immediately. "No, I can't."

"Then trust that she, *they,* did it for good reasons that you don't yet understand."

He gripped the steering wheel tightly. "I know you're right…. But I just hope that we find something today that shines some light on what those reasons were."

"I hope so, too," Kendra agreed, but no matter how the day's venture turned out, she knew that she would not regret spending the day with him. She couldn't help feeling that time was running out, and she selfishly determined to relish every moment that she had with this man who had come to mean so much to her.

* * *

By mutual agreement, they made only one stop on their way to Fort Worth, to refuel and purchase a map of the city. Jack intended to go about this venture in as methodical a fashion as possible. He'd let his emotions get the better of him last time, and this time he meant to exhaust every possible avenue to uncover the truth about his family. Besides, he didn't want to come away fearing that Grayson could have done a better job.

At almost precisely ten o'clock that morning, they pulled into the dusty parking lot of a tired-looking, brick building in the modest, aging neighborhood where Jack's family had once lived. The Anytime Coffee Shop advertised Breakfast Anytime in flashing neon letters mounted in the cloudy front window.

"Don't know about you," Jack said, "but I could eat a whole hog right about now."

Kendra laughed. "Some bacon and eggs would be great."

"Let's just hope the joint is cleaner inside than out," Jack muttered, opening the truck door. Time had reduced the once-paved parking lot to patches of tarry gravel that crunched under his boot heels as he moved around the front of the truck to help Kendra down to the ground. Giving in to impulse, he laid a possessive hand against the small of her back and ushered her into the building.

The tiny, L-shaped dining area offered only seven

or eight small, chrome-legged tables. A counter down the center of the room provided several extra seats. A fellow in a mechanic's uniform occupied one of the stools, hunching silently over a cup of coffee. A pair of Hispanic women with an apple-cheeked infant in a cumbersome carrier occupied the table in the corner, chattering softly over the remains of their meal. A gravelly voice called out from the kitchen.

"Be right with you."

"Thanks," Jack called back, following Kendra to a nearby table.

He pulled out an old-fashioned chrome-and-vinyl chair, saw her seated, then walked around to take the seat opposite her. She passed him one of a pair of yellowed menus encased in heavy plastic. The offerings were few and straightforward: eggs and bacon, eggs and ham, eggs and steak, eggs and sausage. The place looked clean, if utilitarian, however, and that would do. Besides, he sat across from the most beautiful woman imaginable.

What else could a fellow want with breakfast?

A beefy, balding man wearing a stained bib apron and an envelope cap over jeans and a black T-shirt dropped a plate in front of the mechanic at the counter before filling two small glasses with water. He carried both in one large hand as he clumped over to slide them onto the table between Jack and Kendra.

"What'll you have?" he asked unceremoniously,

planting his hands at his thick waist. An older man with bags under his eyes and prominent red veins in the bulb of his nose, he seemed none too friendly.

Jack decided to stick with the tried and true and ordered scrambled eggs accompanied by a slab of ham and toast. "I've had plenty of coffee, though," he said, "so just orange juice."

Kendra chose orange juice and scrambled eggs, too, but asked for bacon. "Crisp, please."

Their host did not so much as reply before turning away and clopping back to the kitchen. Jack lifted his eyebrows at Kendra, who shrugged. Okay, so the service couldn't be called stellar, but maybe the food would make up for that. While they sipped their water and waited for their meal, Jack got out his city map, unfolding and refolding it to showcase the immediate area and fit it onto the tiny Formica tabletop.

"The house is about here," he said, tapping a spot on the map. "I thought we'd start with the houses that we missed last time, but we'll avoid Patty Earl since I've already spoken to her."

"Is she the one who told you that Brian might not be your dad?" Kendra asked.

Jack nodded. "She claims that her late husband, Joe, fathered Grayson and me but that Mom wouldn't marry Joe because Brian was the better catch."

"That doesn't sound like the woman you and Violet describe," Kendra commented.

"No, it doesn't," Jack agreed, "but then I wouldn't have believed that she had two other children, either."

Kendra laid her hand over his and squeezed. "There has to be a good reason why she didn't tell you."

"And maybe we'll discover it today," Jack said hopefully.

Kendra smiled. "Whatever happens," she promised. "I'm here for you."

"For now," he qualified softly.

Oh, how she wanted to argue with that. If only she could promise forever. If only… But it wouldn't do any good to pretend. Besides, she desperately wanted to make Jack see that living in the truth was the best anyone could do.

Chapter Twelve

The mechanic threw a few bills on the counter and rose to leave, calling out, “See you later, Harv.”

“Yeah. Later,” came the rumbling reply.

The guy was barely out the door before “Harv” appeared to pocket the bills. With a disinterested glance at Jack and Kendra, he returned to the kitchen.

“I wonder how long he’s been in business here,” Jack mused.

She met his eyes.

“You think he’s the owner?”

“Wouldn’t surprise me.”

“Harv” carried two plates out of the kitchen and over to the table. Jack folded up the map and pushed it aside so the plates could be put down. Pulling two plastic bottles of juice from his apron pockets, he placed those on the table, as well, then started to turn away.

"This place been here long?" Jack asked conversationally.

The man dropped a cool, pale gray gaze on Jack, answering tersely, "'Bout forty years."

Jack opened his mouth to ask if he was the owner, but the man turned his back and walked away before Jack could get the words out.

"O-kay," Jack drawled.

Kendra inclined her head sympathetically, saying, "Food looks good."

It did, actually. The eggs were fluffy and light, the ham juicy, the bacon crisp, the toast lightly browned. While they ate, their unfriendly host banged around the kitchen then came out to perch on the end stool at the counter and peruse a newspaper while nursing a cup of coffee.

Jack wolfed down his meal, pushed aside his plate and went back to the map, thinking aloud. "There's an old market here," he pointed out. "We can ask there if we strike out with the neighbors. Also, I noticed a gas station and mechanic's shop that looks like it's been around a while, we could try that."

"I saw a dry cleaner's and a pharmacy that look well established, too," Kendra said. "Might find someone who knew Belle and Brian Wallace there."

Jack caught movement from the corner of his eye and turned his head in that direction. Harv had swiveled around on the stool to stare at them, but as soon as Jack looked in his direction, the man got up and headed back to the kitchen. Had he overheard their conversation, and, if so, did that have anything to do with his hasty retreat?

"Last but not least," Jack added, frowning speculatively, "there's a church a couple blocks over. Maybe someone there knew us."

"Good plan," Kendra said.

He abandoned his useless suspicions to smile at her. "Might as well get to it."

They walked over to the cash register to pay out, but their host did not materialize as expected, so Jack dinged the flat bell sitting next to the old-fashioned machine.

Harv came out, scowling and wiping his hands on a towel. "Doing everything myself," he grumbled, taking Jack's money.

He plucked the change from the drawer and dumped it on the counter before striding back into the kitchen. Jack left enough for a tip, took the rest and ushered Kendra to the door, something telling him that Harv couldn't wait to be shed of them. Jack told himself that he was being paranoid, but he couldn't shake the feeling that the taciturn man knew something about his family.

It seemed an inauspicious start to the day, and unfortunately, things did not get better. Ten of a dozen residents opened their doors to Jack and Kendra, but not one of them admitted to remembering a family named Wallace who had once lived on the street. Most were renters who had lived in the area only months.

Downcast, they began canvassing the local businesses. A Mexican chain had recently taken over the local grocery, installing new management and employees, so no one there could help. The owners of the dry-cleaning store, though very friendly, were also fairly new on the scene. Jack and Kendra waited nearly forty minutes to speak to the pharmacist, who remembered a young family from long ago with two sets of twins but couldn't recall their names or any other details. The owner and operator of the combination gasoline station and mechanic's shop turned out to be the son of the recently deceased original proprietor, but all he could tell them was that business was bad and getting worse. Neither the very young pastor nor the middle-aged secretary at the quaint little church could tell them anything.

"Perhaps if you came back on Sunday and spoke to some of our long-term members..." the pastor suggested.

Jack and Kendra gave their regrets and went on their way. As soon as they were back in the truck, Kendra proposed that he give Patty Earl another try.

Jack grit his teeth over the prospect. He didn't know why, but he hated to talk to Mrs. Earl. Something about the embittered widow saddened him, or maybe what she'd said about Belle and Brian saddened him. He found the whole thing distasteful and worrisome.

"Maybe we should pray about it," Kendra suggested softly, and Jack's spirit rose instantly.

"I'd like that," he said, reaching for her hand. Threading their fingers together over the center console, they bowed their heads. "Lord, I—I felt strongly that I ought to come here and do this thing," he began. "I don't know why we haven't found any answers. Maybe it was all just wishful thinking on my part. Now, I just don't know what to do. Can Mrs. Earl help me?" Jack instantly understood that he wouldn't know the answer to that question until he spoke to Patty Earl. "Guess I'll give it a shot and leave what happens to You," Jack said. "Thanks for listening. Amen." He immediately put the key into the truck's ignition switch.

"You're going over there, aren't you?" Kendra said.

Jack nodded. "Yep."

Three minutes later, they stood side by side on the porch in front of Mrs. Earl's pristine little house. She opened the door within seconds after Jack knocked.

"You!" she exclaimed before turning her frown on Kendra. "What do you want now?" Before he could answer, she barked, "I don't know that one, and I don't want to."

"I just want to ask you some more questions about—" Jack began.

"Ain't answering no more questions," she snapped, closing the door in his face.

Jack blinked and shifted his weight before looking at Kendra, who said only, "Well."

Shaking his head, Jack turned away, muttering, "I haven't trusted her from the first."

"I don't blame you," Kendra muttered.

Shaking his head, Jack thought that they'd run out of options, but then a sudden notion took hold of him. "Come on," he said. "We're going back to that coffee shop."

Kendra didn't ask why he wanted to do such a thing, which was good because he couldn't have told her why. He only knew that should be his next—and final—stop of the day. Jack wheeled the truck through the small neighborhood and out onto the main thoroughfare to the Anytime Coffee Shop. The dusty parking lot sat empty, so he parked right in front of the building.

As if sensing his urgency, Kendra bailed out the instant that he killed the engine and waited to fall in behind him as he strode for the door. Harv got up off the stool as soon as the bell over the door jangled. His pale eyes widened.

"We're closing," he announced gruffly, heading for the kitchen.

"Thought you were open twenty-four hours a day," Jack said, striding over to lean a forearm against the countertop. "Isn't that what 'Breakfast Anytime' means?"

Harv cleared his throat. "The night shift called in sick…."

"But it's only four o'clock in the afternoon," Jack pointed out. "Are you telling me that you've been here since four in the morning?"

"I'm not telling you anything," Harv snarled, moving forward again. "Now, get out."

Jack stood his ground. "You own this place, don't you?" Jack asked.

"What of it?"

"And you've been here for the better part of the forty years it's been open, haven't you?" he added.

"I got nothing to say!"

"About what?" Jack prodded. "About Isabella and Brian Wallace?" He stepped closer in the hope of softening the old man. "Isabella's my mother."

"Out!" Harv roared, jabbing a thick finger at the door. "Get out before I call the cops and have you thrown out!"

"Come on, Jack," Kendra urged, hooking her hand in the crook of his elbow. Jack let her pull him toward the door without once taking his eyes off the other man. Why did just the mention of Isabella and Brian Wallace have this fellow so riled up?

Kendra pulled open the door and tugged Jack through it. At the same time, Harv lunged forward and practically shoved Jack out in his urgency to close and lock that door. He shut off all the lights for good measure and disappeared into the back of the building, while Jack stood there watching through the grimy window and shaking his head.

A battered sedan had joined the pickup truck in

the parking lot, and it's driver, a thin, middle-aged man in boots, jeans and a plain white, long-sleeved shirt, got out. He flipped a friendly wave at Jack and Kendra as he slipped past them on his way to the door. Finding it locked, he first looked down in surprise before trying again to push his way through, only to back off and scratch his graying head.

He stepped up to the glass and peered inside, cupping his hands around his eyes. "What's going on, Harv?" he called out. "Let me in!"

"He's closed," Kendra said helpfully.

The man stared as if she'd suddenly grown a third eyeball. "Closed! Earl never closes!"

"Earl?" Jack echoed. "I thought his name was Harv."

"Yeah. Harvey Earl."

Jack staggered back a step, coming up against the bumper of his own truck. "Y-you wouldn't know, would you, if he's any kin to Joe and Patty Earl?"

"He's Joe's father, but Joe, he's been dead for some time now."

Jack's jaw dropped. "He lied to me."

"I never lied!" the fellow exclaimed.

"No." Jack shook his head, focusing. "I didn't mean you. You've been…helpful. Thank you."

"No problem," the man muttered, walking uncertainly back toward his car. "Strange doings. The Anytime closed, folks calling folks liars…"

"Wait!" Jack called, just as the man started to

slide behind the steering wheel of his sedan. "Do you, by any chance, know anything about a family, who lived around here fifteen to twenty years ago, with the name Wallace? Brian and Isabella Wallace. They had four kids, two sets of identical twins, a pair of boys and a pair of baby girls."

The man considered then shook his head. "Naw, I sure don't. Did they live north or south of this here street?"

"North."

"Well, there you go. I live south. Don't never go on the north side."

Bitter disappointment swamped Jack as he watched the fellow drive off. Kendra stepped up to his side and laid a hand between his shoulder blades.

"I'm sorry, Jack."

Sorry. He was sick of sorry. Whirling around, he stomped over to the door of the breakfast diner. Doubling up his fists, he aimed a trio of shuddering blows on the glass, shouting, "I want to talk to you, old man!"

Harvey Earl's head appeared in the kitchen doorway. "Go away before I call the cops," he blustered.

"Call them," Jack said. "You can tell them why you threw out your grandson."

Harv seemed to think on that before easing forward to skirt the counter and approach the door. When he hesitated, Jack rattled the door. Finally, the old man reached out and threw the bolt, stepping back as Jack pulled open the heavy glass panel.

"I—I didn't know who you are," Harv offered lamely.

"You knew," Jack accused, aware that Kendra followed on his heels as he advanced into the room. "What are you so afraid of?"

Harvey looked away briefly, then mumbled, "I ain't afraid of anything. It's just…" He shook his head. "I don't want no trouble with the Wallaces."

"Colby," Jack said coldly. "My name is Jack Colby. I don't even know Brian Wallace."

The old man's eyes narrowed. "I heard he took one of you boys and Isabella took the other."

"That's right. They split two sets of twins when they went their separate ways. The question is why they did it."

Harvey tilted his head. "Your ma still ain't talking?"

"She's in a coma," Jack informed him, the tragedy of it draining away the last of his anger.

"That's too bad," Harv said. "My Joe was sure sweet on that girl. I told him he was wasting his time, but…" A slyness came over Harvey's face. "Maybe she had more time for him than I thought."

"You're not sure?" Jack pressed.

Harvey appeared to choose his words carefully. "Joe always claimed you boys were his. Didn't have no reason to doubt him."

Somehow, Jack found that difficult to believe.

"If that's so, why didn't you try to claim Grayson and me?"

"Didn't know where to find you, now did I?" Harvey returned smoothly. He seemed to relax then, putting on a smile that Jack supposed was meant to pass for affable. "Who's this Colby fellow your mother hooked up with, anyway?"

Stiffening, Jack frowned. "There is no *Colby fellow*. It's just a name."

"I hear tell there's a ranch, though, a big ranch."

"It didn't come from anyone named Colby," Jack said, suddenly feeling that he ought to watch his words. He changed the subject, asking baldly, "Do you know why my folks split up, why they broke apart the family?"

Harvey Earl rubbed his chin with a beefy paw as if calculating his reply. Finally, he shook his head. "Can't say as I do. But that don't mean we can't be family. I wouldn't mind seeing that ranch of yours."

"I bet you would," Jack murmured, feeling an urgent hand on his shoulder. He turned, but no one stood behind him. Kendra waited to one side, observing warily. Suddenly, Jack had to get out of there. Reaching out to snag her hand, he said, "This was a mistake."

He shoved through the door, towing her behind him.

Harvey Earl followed them, calling, "Don't be a stranger now."

But a stranger was exactly what Jack felt like,

even to himself. He shuddered and felt Kendra's free hand skim up his arm.

"Are you okay?"

"Of course I'm not okay," he snapped. "How can I be okay when that hateful old man in there could be my grandfather?"

"He's not," Kendra stated flatly, squeezing his arm. "Even if it does turn out that Joe Earl is your biological father, that man in there is *not* your grandfather."

Jack clenched his jaw. "You don't know that."

"I know what a grandfather is," she insisted.

"You don't even remember your own grandfather or if you even have one," Jack couldn't help pointing out.

Clutching his hand with both of hers, Kendra said softly, "I know what a grandfather should be, and Harvey Earl is no one's grandfather. Certainly not yours."

"I pray to God you're right," Jack muttered, starting blindly toward his truck. *Please, God. Please let her be right.*

"I'm so sorry, Jack," Kendra said for perhaps the sixth or seventh time as the pickup truck sped along the highway headed west toward Grasslands and the ranch. She felt just awful at the way things had turned out. "I really thought we'd learn something useful today."

"We learned that we should've stayed home," Jack grumbled.

Kendra felt a pang of regret. "I can't accept that," she countered softly.

At least they'd had the day together. For her, that meant a great deal.

"All I ever come away with is more questions," Jack snapped. "And frankly, if that old man back there is my grandfather, I don't even want to know."

"I can't blame you for that," Kendra admitted. Meeting Harvey Earl had cast a pall on the entire trip. "But I still think that learning about your past is important."

"Is it?" Jack demanded, slicing her with a glance. "You're still keen to learn about your past, are you?"

"Yes," she whispered, "and no."

Yes because she desperately wanted to know who she was, if she had family, friends, anyone who loved her, and no because bad things could be lurking in her past—and because once she knew who and what she was, she'd almost certainly have to leave Jack. She had to accept the fact that, whatever her name, she could not be from around Grasslands; otherwise, someone would have recognized her by now.

They rode in silence for more than twenty minutes before Jack spoke again. "I don't blame you because the day didn't turn out well."

"It's okay if you do," she told him, smiling wanly. "This whole thing was my idea."

"I wanted to do it," he admitted after a moment, "but I wish I hadn't."

She bowed her head, telling herself that she had no right to be wounded. In his shoes, she'd feel the same way. For her the day had been little more than an excuse to spend a protracted amount of time in Jack's company. For him, the considerations had been different. He wanted to know who his father was and why his family had split. How else could he accept having a twin, a sister and possibly a half brother about whom he'd known nothing? Without the truth, how did he reconcile the idea that his mother had abandoned half of her children? The amnesiac charity case along for the ride couldn't possibly figure into all that. Still, it hurt that having her with him didn't mean as much to Jack as being with him meant to her.

"I only want you to make peace with your past," she managed after a moment.

"Look," he said, sounding as if he'd given this serious thought recently, "my situation isn't really like yours. I know who I am, and that's what matters. I used to think that I needed to know who my father was and maybe my grandparents. Now, I know how foolish that was. My mother tried to tell me to let it be, but I wouldn't listen, and just look at her.... I don't need to know anything else. I don't *want* to know."

"You can't tell me these questions about your past

haven't been eating at you," Kendra began, but he cut her off with the slash of one hand.

"Not anymore. I'm done. The past is the past. Let it stay there."

Sighing inwardly, Kendra swallowed all of the arguments that she wanted to make. She knew Jack well enough now to realize that he would need time to process his thoughts and feelings before he could hear any sort of opinion on the matter. She decided that she would give him the space he needed. In the meantime she would ponder the situation at length, and ask God to give her the right words to help Jack make peace with his past. She couldn't bear the thought of him careening through life with his heart closed to the truth or, worse yet, those who most loved him.

The sunlight faded, and as the darkness deepened so did the silence. Kendra turned her face to the night-blackened window and tried to escape her concerns by blanking her mind. Somewhere along the way, she fell asleep.

The next thing she knew, she was being shaken awake.

"We're here," Jack said huskily.

Kendra straightened, sucking in a deep, cleansing breath, and looked around her. He had parked the truck next to Maddie's little car in front of the house.

"I'll walk you in," Jack said, sliding out of the truck.

Stretching, Kendra frowned at his choice of words,

but she put on a smile as he opened her door for her. He backed away as she stepped down.

"You're not staying, are you?"

He shook his head wearily. "I ought to check on some things at my place. Might as well stay there for the night."

When he turned toward the ranch house, she had little choice but to fall in beside him. "Don't you want to tell your sisters what happened today?" she asked.

"Nothing to tell."

"Jack, please," she began.

"You get some rest," he interrupted. "I, for one, am too tired to make sense right now, and despite that little nap, I know you're the same."

She couldn't argue with that. Besides, hadn't she decided, just before slipping off to sleep, that she would ponder and pray before trying to reason with him? They drew up at the door. He reached around her and opened it.

"I'm sorry for how things turned out," she said, pausing before going inside, "but I'm glad I got to go with you today."

He stood there for a long moment, obviously warring with himself. Finally, he nodded, but then he backed up, tucking his hands into his back pockets. "Good night."

She felt a flare of panic, as if he was telling her goodbye, but that couldn't be the case. He would never leave this ranch, so until she did, they would be in some proximity. She would see him again. Of course, she would see him again, if only in church tomorrow. Relieved by that thought, she smiled warmly.

"Good night, Jack."

"Lock the door behind you," he ordered. "We've got crazy people leaving weird gifts and notes around. Better to be safe than sorry."

"Yes…all right," she said.

He backed away, keeping eye contact with her until she stepped over the threshold. Then he turned away and strode swiftly back to his truck. Kendra waited until he got inside and started up the engine. Then, blinded by the headlights as he backed up the truck and turned it toward the drive, she closed the door and set the lock.

The house felt still and empty. She quickly ascertained that both Violet and Maddie were out, probably with their respective fiancés. It was Saturday night, after all. Sighing, Kendra made her way to her room. She took a long bath and tried to read, but she couldn't seem to concentrate, so she tried to sleep instead, but sleep took its time in coming, despite her physical and mental weariness.

She woke looking forward to church. Not only would worship soothe her soul, she would see Jack and be able to assess how he fared after yesterday's disappointment. Knowing that, she took special care in dressing, washing her hair and brushing it dry.

Breakfast proved to be a bit of a trial, as she had

to explain to Violet and Maddie that she and Jack had learned nothing beyond the fact that the late Joe Earl's father, Harvey, seemed a strangely unfriendly, even hostile, sort to run a coffee shop. The twins could not hide their disappointment, and both seemed disturbed by the fact that Jack had chosen to once again spend the night elsewhere.

Kendra tried not to take their misgivings too seriously, but she knew that she wouldn't relax until she saw him again and could discern his mood. She prayed that he would be in a sunnier frame of mind. It wasn't as if anything had been taken away, after all. It was simply that nothing of any significance had been added to their knowledge. Fortified with that argument, Kendra rode into Grasslands with the twins in Violet's SUV.

Even before Violet parked the little sport-utility vehicle, however, it became apparent that Kendra would be a fifth wheel if she stayed with the sisters. Landon and Ty waited for the twins on the walkway in front of the church. Spying Sadie Johnson, the church secretary, standing alone near the door, Kendra excused herself to speak to the shy young woman.

"Hello, again," she said, going up to stand at Sadie's side.

Sadie ducked her head, replying softly, "Hello."

Kendra glanced around to find that Violet had linked arms with Landon, while Maddie and Ty clasped hands. Surveying the parking lot, she failed to see Jack's truck, so she turned a smile on Sadie and made a forthright admission.

"I could use some company."

Sadie's eyes rounded almost comically. "Oh. A-all right." Gathering music began to emanate from the sanctuary just then, and those few standing around started moving. "I guess we should go in," Sadie suggested meekly.

Kendra smiled and nodded, matching her steps to those of the slender young woman at her side. "Where do you usually sit?"

"Up front," Sadie told her, picking up her pace a bit. "I like to see and hear…everything."

Kendra noticed that as she spoke, Sadie's gaze darted to the pastor, who sat opposite the piano, to one side of the altar.

"That's fine," Kendra said, wondering if the timid church secretary had developed a crush on the affable young preacher, who was handsome in his own wholesome, boy-next-door fashion.

They wound their way to the front pew, which they had to themselves. Nevertheless, Sadie squeezed into the corner nearest the wall. Kendra took a moment to survey the crowd, looking for Jack, but she finally had to accept that he had not yet arrived. Violet sent her a questioning little shrug, but Kendra merely waved then took a seat next to Sadie.

The worship service did soothe her, but Kendra kept praying silently that Jack had slipped in behind her. Of course, she couldn't turn around to look. It was impossible to say immediately afterward if he'd been in attendance, owing to the glut of bodies that spilled into the aisle and out the door. By virtue of having sat on the front pew, she and Sadie were the last two to file out through the back of the church. The pastor greeted her with a patient smile and firm handshake, but Kendra noticed that he took a slow, easy pleasure in speaking to Sadie. Kendra felt compelled to give them some privacy and took herself off after a whispered farewell to her shy friend.

Violet and Maddie met her on the walkway, identical looks of concern on their faces. They didn't have to tell her. She already knew instinctively.

"Jack didn't show up for church."

That meant, of course, that his withdrawal this time was very serious.

And it was all her fault.

Chapter Thirteen

As a rule, Jack did not miss church on Sunday, but he couldn't yet bring himself to face his sisters with another failure, and he clearly could not trust himself around Kendra. She drew him as no other woman ever had. Imagine how she might affect him if he actually knew her name!

Meanwhile, he felt…betrayed. By his mother, by his father—whoever he was—by Kendra, who had been so sure that going to Fort Worth was the right thing to do and even, in a small corner of his heart, by God. *Can't a guy get a break?* He then ran through a long litany of unjust and downright absurd tribulations.

His mother lay in a coma due to an accident that he had caused.

His supposed father had somehow become lost in South Texas and could be seriously ill.

His *alleged* father seemed to have been a somewhat shady character, judging by his own father and widow.

He had a twin he'd never known existed, let alone met.

Instead of the one sister with whom he'd grown up, he had *two* sisters, also twins.

In the background hovered the possibility of a half brother. Or not.

Add to that last year's disappointment with Tammy.

And last but not least, he couldn't get a certain beautiful, young amnesiac out of his head.

It didn't seem to matter that he didn't even know who she was—or that she might already be promised to some other man. He'd never felt about another woman the way he felt about her, which just proved how perverse his heart could be.

Well, she'd be gone soon; that being the case, he should just keep his distance, even if it meant staying away from church.

Maybe it was petty of him, but he didn't particularly want to be around his sisters and their fiancés, either. Landon seemed to find a million little reasons to touch Violet, and Ty was the same with Maddie. Jack didn't begrudge them their happiness, but he didn't see why he had to have his nose rubbed in it.

Moreover, he was sick and tired of hearing Maddie go on about Grayson. His twin might be some hotshot undercover cop, but Maddie talked about

Gray as if he was all that and a bag of chips—while he, Jack, couldn't find the answer to a single question about their shared past.

It galled.

It hurt.

It made him want to lash out, and that alone was reason enough to keep his distance.

Still, he half expected someone—Violet or Kendra or even Maddie—to show up on Sunday afternoon, if only to check on him. When it became apparent that wouldn't happen, his mood blackened. Waking up in pain on Monday morning didn't help one bit.

Stretching his sore, aching muscles, he decided the time had come to bring in some comforts of home. He'd spent too many nights in a sleeping bag on the floor, which seemed stupid since the house was now ready for furniture, at least in the rooms he would use.

As he put the finishing touches on the paint in the master bedroom, he considered his options. He was pretty sure that his mom kept Uncle James's old bedroom suite in the attic at the main house. Jack couldn't see any reason why she wouldn't want him to use it. Someone ought to. Then there was that living-room set he'd bought on sale last year to replace the old one at the ranch foreman's house, only to discover that his mom and Ty had already beat him to it. Used but clean and in good shape, the stuff would fit his needs nicely. He'd require some dishes, too, as well as a few linens, and a television would be welcome. He would have to do some shopping, but so be it. Might as well plan on picking up a few groceries, too.

His plan decided, he made a few calls to arrange help then cleaned his painting tools, timing his arrival at the main house just in time for lunch. Lupita feigned shock at seeing him.

"Fancy seeing you here."

Jack rolled his eyes at her then leaned in to kiss her cheek, his gaze going involuntarily to the figure behind her. Kendra gave him a tremulous smile.

"Jack."

He tried not to be happy to see her. He really did. Switching his gaze to the table, he headed straight there—and found a meager lunch of soup and salad waiting.

Behind him, Lupita said wryly, "I'll make you a sandwich."

"Yeah, thanks," he mumbled.

"We didn't know you'd be here," Kendra explained, going to the cabinet for a plate and bowl. "When it's just me and Lupita, we tend to eat light."

Jack knew that Violet often stayed in town at this time of year, overseeing the farm store. After the end of harvest, she'd be around more often during the day.

"Maddie's working at the newspaper, I guess," he said.

Kendra shook her head. “She said something about planning a picnic.”

“Oh. Right.” Maddie was on the planning committee for the monthly picnic on the church grounds. They went on as long as weather permitted, so the next could be the last one for some months. Jack looked to Lupita, remembering the arrangements he’d made that morning. “Better put together a couple extra sandwiches. Some of the boys are coming up to help me move stuff around.”

As if on cue, a hail of knocks fell on the side door. Jack strode into the hallway to let the “boys” in. Beating dust from their jeans with two of the most disreputable hats ever seen, the pair shined the toes of their boots on their calves before stepping up into the house.

“What’s up, boss?” one of them asked as they followed him back down the hall.

“Just need a couple extra pairs of hands,” he answered carefully. “Sit yourselves down and have a bite of lunch first, though.”

He couldn’t help noticing, with some irritation, that the two cowboys greeted Kendra like a long-time friend. It didn’t help that she rushed to set down extra plates and bowls, literally foregoing her own lunch in order to feed the men. Jack scowled, but she hastily assured him that there was more where that had come from, and Lupita agreed, plopping down a plate stacked with sandwiches. The women insisted that the men go ahead and eat while they scrabbled together their own meal. To Jack's chagrin, the hands fell on the food like they'd been starved for salad, vegetable soup and roast-beef sandwiches.

Lupita did have more soup, but instead of salad, she and Kendra made do with sliced apples, toast and bits of beef. When Kendra carried her food to the table, Jack nearly bit off the arm of the fellow who jumped up to pull out a chair for her, but he himself kept to his seat, even though that went against every gentlemanly precept he'd ever been taught. He managed, just barely, not to growl when Kendra smiled in gratitude at the cowboy's gallantry. The remainder of the meal, while brief, did not improve Jack's mood. Wolfing down his own food, he did not wait for the hands to complete their seemingly unhurried meals before ordering them up the stairs.

"Can I help?" Kendra asked, rising as the men did.

Jack glowered down at her. "No."

The stricken look on her face yanked the breath right out of his lungs, but he made himself turn away and lead the men from the room.

They accessed the attic via a door on the upstairs landing. Jack found the bedroom suite covered by sheets and dusty boxes. After moving the boxes aside, they maneuvered the pieces—a bedstead, two side tables and a tallboy dresser—out onto the landing. Only as he carried out the bed rails did it occur to him that he was going to need a mattress and box springs. His shopping list grew.

By the time the last piece went down the stairs and out the door, Kendra and Lupita both had figured out what was going on. Kendra, however, took the bull by the horns, accusing, "You're moving out."

"Naw," he said, avoiding her hazel gaze. It wasn't as if he'd packed up his clothes and personal belongings, after all. "Just getting the other house together a little bit."

One of the hands asked what Jack wanted them to do next. He had them load the bedroom suite into the bed of the old range truck they'd driven in, then he directed one of them to drive that truck and its load over to his place. The other man would ride over to the storage shed with him in his truck.

"Jack, please don't," Kendra pleaded.

"Look," he said, too cheerfully, "I'm just sprucing up the other place. I mean, this is what I've been working toward, you know?"

"Talk to your sisters about it first," Kendra encouraged.

Frowning, he tried to ameliorate his need to snap at her by keeping his tone even. "I don't need anyone's permission to furnish my own house. Besides, it's just a few things."

He saw the tears brimming in her eyes and turned away, knowing that if he gave in now, he would never do this, not so long as it brought her pain.

God knew that he didn't want to hurt her. In a very real way, that's what he was trying to avoid. For both of them. If he didn't keep some distance between them, they would grow entirely too close. Then when her memory returned and she left town, they would both suffer.

He couldn't bear to think of her leaving, so he wouldn't. In fact, he had a long list of things that he didn't want to think about, and keeping busy was the only way he knew to do it. Stubbornly determined to stay the course, he went over to his truck and climbed in with the remaining ranch hand.

Even the sight of Kendra standing there with a look of utter sadness on her face did not deter him. Starting the engine, he backed out the truck and aimed it toward a line of outbuildings in the distance. He and the hand picked up the living-room set, along with an old rocker and a battered trunk that Jack intended to use as a coffee table. He imagined rocking contentedly in front of a cheery fire while reading a book or watching television, and ignored the loneliness that seemed to creep over him.

They arrived at his place to find the other truck waiting. The driver had carried in all the small pieces, including the dresser drawers. As Jack and his two helpers carried the remaining furniture pieces into the house—*his* house—Jack kept seeing Kendra's face. He knew her well enough now to recognize the pain of rejection in her eyes. He told himself that it was for the best, but as he busily went about trying to make a home out of his house, he couldn't pretend that he didn't care.

The problem, of course, was that he cared too much.

Violet plopped down on the foot of Kendra's bed and sighed, following Kendra with her gaze as she padded over to the window seat and perched there.

"Gwen Simmons says that Jack bought pots and pans at the ranch supply store yesterday and a whole box of dishes at the resale shop," Violet reported. "She even claims that he drove up to Amarillo today to buy a mattress."

Kendra nodded, swallowing hard. "I'm so sorry, Violet. This is all my fault. If I hadn't pressured him to go to Fort Worth after the fiasco in South Texas…"

"Now, you stop that," Violet scolded gently. "My brother doesn't bow to pressure. Jack makes up his own mind about everything. He's always been that way. He's always had a tendency to den up like a hibernating bear when he's wounded, confused or angry, but in this case I'm not sure it's such a bad thing. This is the first time he's really shown any interest in making a home out of that old place. Until now, it's been more like a hobby."

Kendra appreciated the absolution. Still, she felt miserable about the whole thing. Even if Violet didn't blame her for her brother's current state of mind, Jack certainly did. Why else was he avoiding her? If she'd needed any more proof that he was keeping his distance from her, he'd certainly given it to her by essentially moving out of this house and into his own. What hurt most, though, was the knowledge that, in avoiding her, he also avoided his family.

She'd never be able to forgive herself if she'd driven Jack away from his family. What if he never found his way back?

How would Jack cope if Joe Earl did turn out to be his father? She feared that Jack would unconsciously distance himself from Violet and Maddie because they happened to be his half sisters rather than the whole sisters that he obviously wanted them to be. If he held himself apart from the family, would he even get to know Grayson or Carter? And what about his mother? Kendra prayed Belle Colby would awaken soon from her coma, but Jack should be there when she did, not off brooding about the mysteries of his past or his imagined guilt.

In some ways, Kendra wanted to shake him until the scales dropped from his eyes and he saw how precious his family was. At the same time, she wanted to wrap her arms around him and simply love him until his pain stopped. Unfortunately, she had no right to do either one.

"I wonder if the big dope even thought to buy a lamp," Violet worried aloud, getting up off the bed. "There are no overhead lights in the downstairs bedroom or the living room, but you know what men are like."

"He'll probably try to make do with a flashlight," Kendra said distractedly.

Violet laughed. "Probably. Maybe I'll buy him a lamp."

"That would be nice," Kendra commented idly.

Violet narrowed her eyes, obviously thinking, and shifted her stance. "Tell you what," she said. "I'll buy the lamp if you'll deliver it to him."

Surprised, Kendra blinked. "Oh, but how would I—"

"This is a busy time of year for me," Violet went on, "but I can find a few minutes to get around town and do a bit of shopping if you can deliver it to Jack."

"I'm always glad to help," Kendra began, "but—"

"That's great!" Violet flashed a smile. "I'll make it a table lamp, something small enough to be easily managed."

"Well, that's fine," Kendra said with thinly veiled exasperation, "but how am I going to get it there?"

Violet shrugged and moved toward the door. "We'll pray on it. Something will work out."

Kendra gave up and agreed. "All right… If you say so."

Although she'd agreed to Violet's request, she honestly didn't see how she could deliver anything to Jack or anyone else. Even if she'd had a vehicle, she couldn't drive without a license. More than likely, what would eventually happen was that Maddie or one of the hands or even Landon, would deliver the lamp to Jack. Still, she would pray about the matter.

Halfway through the door, Violet paused and extracted something from the hip pocket of her jeans. She looked down at it then turned back to Kendra, holding out her hand.

"I almost forgot," she said, "I have something for you."

Kendra stared at the tiny phone in Violet's hand for several seconds. "I—I can't take that. You and your family have done more than enough for me as it is."

"It's just a loan," Violet insisted. "Mom isn't using it, so you might as well."

"Oh, I couldn't take your mother's phone. That's too personal, too…"

"I backed up all the info then deleted everything but a few phone numbers," Violet told her. "It can all be restored when Mom's ready to use it again. Meanwhile, you'll have access to GPS, the internet, weather info." She chuckled. "And a phone, of course."

Kendra bit her lip, considering, then shook her head. "I wouldn't feel right."

"And what happens if you're working down at the barn all alone and, say, a horse steps on your foot and breaks it?" Violet asked, pushing the phone at Kendra. "I know that I'll feel better if you have a way to call for help."

"I can't very well argue with that," Kendra conceded, lifting her hand to accept the small phone.

Violet smiled. "You keep that until Mom wakes up or you remember who you are. Meanwhile, I'll go lamp shopping."

Kendra nodded uncertainly. "Thank you. I appreciate your kindness."

On her way out the door again, Violet murmured, "It was Jack's idea, actually. He pointed out that you had to come back to the house to call the vet the other day. We thought this might be a solution." She flipped her hand in a farewell wave before sweeping through the door.

Kendra stared at the small, rectangular phone. Oh, she was going to miss this place and the friends she had made here. How unfair it seemed to accept such kindnesses and then, once her memory returned, to simply go back to her former life. But what other choice did she have? She clearly did not live around Grasslands or someone would have recognized her by now, and presumably she had another life—a real life—elsewhere.

For the umpteenth time, she'd tried to imagine what that meant—a job, a home, friends, family, possibly fiancé, or even… No, she couldn't believe that she had a husband waiting for her somewhere. The veil convinced her of that. She couldn't conceive of a circumstance that would have led her to rush away in a long veil and blue jeans *after* a wedding. It had to have been *before* the wedding, *if* a wedding had even been in the offing.

Perhaps she had been shopping for a wedding veil—and something had happened to send her rushing off. In an unregistered car? With no identification of any kind? To where?

Kendra shook her head, acknowledging a dull ache that had begun behind her eyes. Had she left behind someone who loved her? Or had she run from a loveless life toward something—or someone—she couldn't remember? And why couldn't she remember?

Surely, God ought to restore her memory and answer all these questions that had been nagging her for weeks. She just could not fathom what He might be doing or why. He surely had a purpose, though, for bringing her here and into the lives of these people. Might it be, dared she even hope, that He didn't intend her to leave this area?

For the first time, she asked God to return her memories but to also let her at least maintain a connection with the Colbys. Or were they the Wallaces? And how could she leave here without knowing the truth about them all? She knew in her heart of hearts that she could not leave until Jack had made peace with his own past and accepted the truth about his family.

Even then, she couldn't imagine how she could leave.

"Oh, Lord," she whispered, clutching that little

phone, "whatever I've done in my past, whoever, whatever I am, please don't let it cut me off from..." She had meant to say, "my friends" or "these good people," but God knew who she really meant and why, so she just said it. "Please don't let it cut me off from Jack."

The second morning after Violet's visit, Kendra came downstairs to find a lamp standing in the center of the breakfast table. A simple grooved cylinder of wood about a foot tall, it sported a base of rusty horseshoes and a small shade of tanned, hand-tooled leather. A short chain hung from the empty lightbulb socket. Kendra had to admit that it suited both Jack and his house to a tee. Moreover, she would have no problem delivering it, provided she found a means of transportation.

With that problem in mind, Kendra shrugged into a long-sleeved, Western-style blouse, buttoning it over her T-shirt as she left the house through the patio door.

"Morning, boy."

Nipper rose complacently and fell in beside her as she strode down the courtyard. It had become a daily ritual with them. Though obviously independent, the Australian shepherd seemed to have appointed himself to accompany her as she performed her daily chores in and around the barn. Kendra welcomed the company, especially since Jack had made himself so scarce.

They met Lupita as she strolled up from the small house that she shared with her husband. The two women exchanged greetings.

"*Buenos dìas,* Lupita."

"Good morning. Coffee, oatmeal and cinnamon biscuits will be waiting for you when your chores are done."

"Yum," Kendra said, continuing on her way.

The morning held a faint crispness, a little taste of autumn, that made such a warming breakfast sound particularly delicious. Kendra couldn't help wishing that Jack would be there to share it. She wondered what he would have to eat with his coffee that morning. Cold cereal? Plain toast? Lupita insisted that he couldn't so much as scramble an egg. Maybe if she went over early enough, Kenda mused, she could deliver the lamp and fix Jack a bite to eat. The problem was how to get there.

She heard the knicker of a horse inside the barn. Kendra stopped dead in her tracks. Of course! Why hadn't she thought of that earlier? She could ride over to Jack's place. At least, she thought she could.

Excited, she slid open the barn door and slipped inside, leaving Nipper to curl up in a pile of hay just outside the building. A meow drew her gaze downward. Thomasina, the cat, sat at her feet, a tiny bit of mottled yellow-and-gray fluff in her mouth.

"Your kittens!" Kendra exclaimed. "You've had your kittens."

She went down on her haunches to examine the baby cat. Obviously hours, rather than minutes old, it mewled weakly. An attentive mother, Thomasina darted off to safety with her infant. Kendra followed, finding the nest that the cat had made for herself and her four kitties in a wooden box that Kendra had previously filled with bits of straw and several old rags just for this purpose. Laughing, Kendra gingerly examined the babies, noting their markings and weight. It was too early to tell their genders for certain, but in the next few days, she could make a determination. The mama cat dropped what was obviously the runt of the litter beside its mewling, squirming siblings and settled down to nurse. Kendra nudged the still-blind kittens onto teats and watched to make sure that everyone was getting fed before rising to go on her way. She smiled as she went about her business, eager to share the news with Jack.

She made quick work of her chores, racing through the tasks with efficient speed. As she cleaned the stalls of the various horses, she made observations on each. The stallion, which was kept separate from the other mounts, seemed restive. Unsure of her level of expertise in the saddle, she ruled him out completely. One of the geldings had a runny eye, which could mean a minor injury, and the other belonged to Jack. She wouldn't ride that horse without his express permission. Since one of the mares had recently given birth and the other belonged to Belle, Kendra decided to ask Violet if she could ride the remaining mare.

Chapter Fourteen

"You'll have to take Mouse," Violet told Kendra across the breakfast table. "The sorrel has to be re-shod. Besides, Mouse can use the exercise."

"Mouse," Kendra repeated uncertainly. "That's your mother's grulla, isn't it?"

"I think we had this conversation last night," Violet said pointedly.

Kendra shifted. "But I don't think Jack would like for me to ride Mouse."

"Someone needs to," Violet asserted. "The hands have been exercising her, but that horse is used to being ridden regularly. Even Jack realizes that on some level." Smiling, she got to her feet, her breakfast finished. "You will take the phone with you?"

Kendra still felt uneasy about riding Jack's mom's horse, but in the end, her desire to see him won out. Violet had insisted, after all. "Yes, of course."

"All right. If you have any questions or problems

with the horse, ring Ty. His number's in the phone. He'll send someone to help or come himself."

Tamping down her misgivings, Kendra nodded. "Thank you."

Violet just shook her head. "One of these days," she drawled, "you're going to run out of thank-yous. Then we can just get on with things." She threw Kendra a grin and went out.

Kendra finished her own breakfast with unseemly haste then rushed upstairs. She would need to put Uncle James's boots to use at least one more time.

The grulla proved to be a bit testy, so Kendra called Ty in hopes of acquiring another mount. Instead, he came and saddled the mare, programmed the GPS on Kendra's borrowed cell phone, showed her how to use the compass application and tied the lamp to the saddle behind the cantle. After watching her mount and walk the horse around the barn, he advised Kendra to use her knees more, remarking that the grulla had a particularly soft mouth. While striding back to his truck, he advised her to call if she had any problems; then he got in and drove away, leaving a very nervous Kendra behind him.

Gulping, she leaned forward and patted the grulla's graceful neck. "It's you and me now, girl. Let's try not to mess this up."

She gave the horse a nudge and found herself bouncing along at a frisky trot. Within a few moments, she found her seat and the grulla hit an easy lope. Soon, Kendra exulted in the sheer joy of riding, sure that she'd done so many times before this.

Stopping repeatedly to check the GPS and the compass cost time, she began to fear that Jack would have left the house long before she arrived, so she welcomed with great relief the sight of Jack's truck parked in the drive. She didn't realize that Jack was behind the wheel until he opened the door and got out, having caught sight of her on the rise above the house. Smiling, she stood in her stirrups and waved. He reached into the truck for his hat, jamming it onto his head with his usual disregard for its shape. The grulla took advantage of Kendra's inattention and bolted down the hill. Laughing, Kendra patiently drew the horse back until they came to a stop in front of the house.

"I brought you a lamp," she said as Jack stepped forward to grab the cheek piece of the bridle, the brim of his hat obscuring his face. Bailing out of the saddle, she began untying the leather strings that held the lamp in place. "Violet bought it. She didn't think you'd have one." Turning with the lamp in her hands, she beamed a smile at Jack and stretched out her arms. "I think she chose well. Don't you?"

"That's why you got on a horse and rode over here by yourself?" he demanded, not even bothering to look at the lamp.

Dismayed, Kendra looked up into eyes gone from light brown to molten gold flashing with anger. "It was the only way to—"

"And on the one horse I *told* you to stay away from!" he shouted, making the horse dance sideways.

Kendra gaped at him. "I knew you would be concerned, but Violet insisted, and it's fine. There were no prob—"

"This horse nearly killed my mother," Jack roared, "and you expect me to believe that Violet *insisted* you ride her!"

"She did!" Kendra shot back. "She said the grulla needed exercise and the sorrel had to be re-shod."

"Like those are the only two horses we own. I don't think so!"

He let go of the bridle, his arm rising as if to shoo the horse away. Kendra let the lamp fall and reached out, snagging the reins.

"We did just fine on the way over here," she told him hotly, ignoring the way the horse yanked its head. "I can ride just as well as you."

"No one rides any better than my mother," he argued. "And because of that horse she's lying comatose in a hospital."

That reminder of what Belle Colby and her family had suffered made Kendra take a stranglehold on her own temper. "I haven't forgotten," she answered softly. "I pray for her every day."

Grinding his teeth, Jack parked his hands at his waist. Kendra bent and, keeping a grip on the reins with one hand, swept up the lamp with the other.

Relieved to see that it had suffered no harm, she offered it to him again.

"Your sister sent you this."

Jack snatched the gift out of her hand and nodded curtly before plunking it down on the porch behind him. He then turned back to Kendra and held out his hand.

"Give me the reins."

Kendra realized that he intended to confiscate the horse, and the unfairness of that plummeted her. She'd done just fine on the way over here, and Violet *had* insisted that Kendra take this particular mount. In fact, Violet was behind this whole thing. Kendra had ridden over here at Violet's behest to give him that lamp he so callously ignored. She drew back.

"No. You're not angry because you're worried about me riding this horse. Your anger is just another way of avoiding the questions that plague you."

"I'm not avoiding the questions that plague me," he bellowed. "I'm avoiding the *people* who plague me!"

Kendra gasped, pain slicing through her. He meant that he was avoiding *her*. He had moved out of his mother's house just to avoid her. Not his sisters, not his sense of failure or guilt, not the family upheaval, just *her*.

She had known it, of course. What she hadn't realized was how much she'd been hoping for the opposite. Some part of her had held to the hope that she might be collateral damage, that avoiding her was nothing more than a by-product of his attempts to avoid all the rest. She had even thought, God help her, that Jack was coming to feel for her what she felt for him. In truth, though, he felt only irritation and anger.

And she couldn't blame him one bit.

What, after all, had she brought to his life but problems and disappointment? He'd had plenty of those before he'd found her in that wrecked car, but he'd still given her a place to stay, a job and whatever else she'd needed. She'd repaid him with bad advice, all but bullying him into traipsing around Texas in search of answers to questions that Jack didn't even want to ask. If she was him, she'd avoid her, too.

Maybe this was why no one had come looking for her. Maybe Jack wasn't the only one whose life she'd blighted.

Suddenly, all she could think about was getting away from him. Vaulting into the saddle, she wheeled the horse, flapped her legs and held on as the animal took off like a shot. Behind her, Jack yelled her name.

"Kendra! Kendra, come back here!"

She ignored him, urging the grulla up the hill. At the top, she let the horse have its head, instinctively bending low over the saddle horn in order to stabilize her center of gravity. The horse ran for a long time, avoiding pitfalls and outgrowths, none of which amounted to more than blurs in Kendra's tear-filled eyes. Finally, she brought the animal to a halt then kneed it into a walk until it stopped blowing. Meanwhile, she wiped her eyes and calmed herself.

The time she had been dreading had come, the time to leave Grasslands.

She tried to think where she would go and how, but everything seemed to hinge on knowing where she'd come from and why. For some time now, she'd felt that there might be an avenue of information to pursue, but she had been reluctant to suggest it simply because she didn't want to leave Jack. Staying would only bring more heartache, though. Even knowing that he had done everything he could to avoid her and that the past she could not remember could rule out any future for them, she had foolishly fallen in love with him. After what had happened today, she could no longer take shelter at the ranch. She had to take her own advice and look for answers. Now.

Pulling out Belle Colby's little phone, Kendra found that she could, as expected, get on the internet with it. From there, discovering a non-emergency number for the Grasslands Police Department took mere moments. To her surprise, a simple request quickly put her in contact with Sheriff George Cole.

She wanted to know, first of all, if he'd made any headway in identifying her. His reply consisted of a single word.

"Nope."

When she pressed him, he admitted that because no one had reported her missing, he hadn't felt it necessary to search beyond the area indicated by the mileage on the odometer of the vehicle, which demonstrated that it had not been driven outside of the state. Kendra suggested that it might be possible for the obviously new vehicle to have been *trucked* into the state rather than driven. Clearly, George had not thought of that.

Kendra's throat felt tight as she told him that no apology was necessary, then asked him to please access the national databases with the Vehicle Identification Number of the car. By the time she'd finished suggesting that he also check with new car dealers within the driving range of the odometer mileage of the wrecked vehicle, she could barely speak. George promised to get right on it and hung up.

Kendra wiped her eyes again, consulted the GPS and compass of the little phone and turned Mouse toward the barn. Along the way, she poured out her broken heart to God. Knowing that she was a pitiful, red-eyed, runny-nosed sight, she did not go to the house. Instead, after unsaddling, grooming and settling the horse, she climbed the ladder to the hayloft.

Mounted on rollers set in a track on the lip of the loft floor, the ladder shifted side to side slightly as she climbed, but Kendra ignored that little inconvenience and persevered. She reached the shadowy space beneath the roof to find no piles of straw but, rather, stacks of feed bags. Made of heavy paper, some of the bags had been arranged as "furniture," stacked in the shapes of an armless chair, bench and coffee table. An empty soda pop can lay on its side atop the makeshift table.

Given his propensity to escape, Kendra could imagine Jack sitting there, enjoying an hour or two of solitude. One of the ranch hands could have fashioned this little nest, of course, but Kendra couldn't see anyone but Jack, think of anyone but Jack.

Jack, who would never be hers.

She might have seen him for the last time, in fact. Their argument might well be the last conversation they would ever share.

Grief felled her. Stumbling forward, she collapsed upon the crude "bench." For the first time, she truly let herself feel all that was in her heart. She cried out to God, but sobs overtook her, and she could not seem to formulate a coherent thought. As she wept, a fragment of Scripture flowed through her mind.

The Spirit helps us in our weakness. We do not know what we ought to pray for, but the Spirit Himself intercedes for us through wordless groans.

That dose of perspective helped calm her somewhat. Eventually, her sobs dwindled to streams of silent tears. Emotionally exhausted, she struggled to gather her memories around her. With her past a blank, she felt as if she had forgotten everything but Jack, lost everything but her faith. Jack had never been hers, of course, whatever her silly heart wanted to believe, but the thought of losing a single memory of him terrified her. Quite deliberately, she began to relive her time with Jack, the better to hold her only memories close.

She recalled waking to Jack's handsome face in the clinic. As then, his presence had reassured her many times over these past weeks. Feeling again her gratitude at his invitation to stay at the ranch, she replayed their conversations in her mind, detailed the meals they had shared, cataloging his favorite foods. She'd never forget the way he'd handed over the barn chores to her or his confidence in her concern for the heifer. Laughter surprised her as she thought of her first pay envelope and the shopping trip afterward, Uncle James's boots, and her first sight of the old rock house Jack had made his own. She'd never see his house finished now, but she could remember touring it with him and imagining how it would look in the future. Even their disagreements became precious. Closing her eyes, she experienced again the way he'd comforted her, their trips together, that day at his mother's bedside and especially that one overwhelming kiss....

So many memories of the man she loved, each one precious beyond words and enough, hopefully, to last her a lifetime.

"She is just fine," Jack told himself doggedly for perhaps the tenth time since Kendra had ridden madly up the slope outside his house. The words gave him no more comfort spoken aloud than they had before he'd started talking to himself.

Throwing down the rag he was using to wipe the stain from the newel posts, he held out his soiled hands and tried to calm himself. He knew Kendra to be a competent horsewoman. The way she'd ridden down that hill—and up again—had proved her skill. But he couldn't forget that his mother was an expert rider, and she had not only fallen, she had fallen from the very same horse that had carried Kendra. Surely, the same thing couldn't happen twice; yet he could not get the fear of it out of his mind.

That same fear had driven him to snap at Kendra. He felt lousy about that. Now. At the time, he'd been too livid at the risk she'd taken by riding over there on his comatose mother's horse to think clearly. Even knowing that Kendra had come to bring him a gift hadn't cooled his temper. He'd just kept picturing her as he'd seen his mother, and the very possibility of such a thing happening again—to Kendra, of all people—had made him a little crazy.

He'd charged to the top of the rise and stood there watching her gallop away as competently as any rider he'd ever seen. When she'd finally reined the horse to a safe stop, he'd turned and stomped back to the house, doing what he so often did, burying his worry with work. Unfortunately, his concern kept rising up to smack him in the face.

The worst part was that if he'd just asked nicely, she'd have let him turn the horse loose and drive her back to the main house. So, once again, if anything bad happened, it would all be his fault. Sick at heart, he went to the Lord.

"Please let her be safe. I'm sorry for losing my temper again. Please, please don't let it lead to disaster, not for Kendra. She doesn't deserve this on top of everything else."

His own words rose up to mock him then. *"I'm not avoiding questions that plague me! I'm avoiding people who plague me!"*

She didn't deserve that, either. Yes, he had been avoiding her. And, yes, she plagued him. Thoughts of her plagued him every moment, and he did feel some resentment over that, but hurting her had hurt him. He'd tried to tell himself that the whole thing had been a minor spat between friends, but the ache in his chest had only intensified. Horrified by what he'd done, he snatched up the rag he'd been using to stain the woodwork and carried it outside. Moving as quickly as possible, he put away the stain and other tools then scrubbed his hands clean before grabbing his hat and jumping into the truck.

All the way over to the main house, he continued to pray, confessing his fears, failings and lack of faith. Kendra had been right. Instead of trusting God to provide the answers to the questions that bedeviled him, he'd simply tried to ignore them. He had also been avoiding all the people whom he feared he'd disappoint—and all those he feared would disappoint him.

He feared that Maddie would never think as well of him as she did Grayson, especially if she turned out to be his half sister. He feared that Grayson would blame him for their mother's accident and that, despite being twins, they would have nothing in common. He feared that his mother would never wake up, that he might discover his father only to lose him again, that Carter would forever remain a stranger. And that when Kendra left, she would take his heart with her. Suddenly, her leaving seemed less important than her being okay.

"God forgive me for being so self-centered," he prayed, remembering that Christ had been willing to suffer so much more than disappointment for those He loved.

Realizing how foolish he'd been to hide away from the very people who comprised his support system, those dearest to him in all the world, he finally let go of the anger and guilt that had been the true plague on his life. As soon as he'd done that, something unexpected and unappreciated rushed in to fill the void.

Love.

Reaching the house, he left the truck out front and hit the door at a near run, coming across Maddie on her way through the foyer.

"Jack!" she exclaimed, smiling happily. "Glad you're here." She waved a hand, saying, "Come. Come with me. I have good news."

"Kendra's here," he immediately surmised, earning a puzzled look from Maddie as he followed her toward the kitchen.

"Kendra? No. That is, I don't think so. I haven't seen her, anyway."

They entered the kitchen to find Violet leaning against the counter and talking softly with Lupita while the cook put the finishing touches on lunch.

"What are you doing here at this time of day?" he asked his sister, fearing the worst.

Violet shrugged and said coyly, "Just thought I'd come home for lunch. Did Kendra deliver the lamp?"

"Yes, she did," he answered distractedly. "It's perfect. Thank you." Bringing his hands to his waist, he asked, "Have you seen Kendra since then?"

At the same time, Maddie announced, "I have news."

Shaking her head at Jack, Violet smiled at her twin. "What?"

"Grayson is free at last and packing to come to Grasslands!" Maddie exclaimed cheerfully.

Jack felt his heart kick. His twin was coming here. Finally, he would meet his brother. His *brother.* A fierce, unexpected gladness filled Jack. He shoved aside his misgivings and smiled.

"That's excellent. It's really great."

"Oh, man," Violet said with a laugh, "we're going to have two of you around."

"Not quite, but close enough," Maddie teased,

beaming at Jack. "Honestly, Gray's a good guy. You're both going to love him."

"Of course we will," Violet said happily. "After all, we both love *you*."

Though she smiled, Maddie darted a look at Jack, and he knew what she wanted, needed, to hear from him. He felt small and churlish for not having given it to her before this, so he gave it to her now.

"Yes," he said, smiling warmly at Maddie, "and we both love you."

Darting forward, Maddie hugged him. "Thanks, brother mine. That means a lot."

Nodding, he patted her back and felt lighter than he had in some time. As she danced away, he cleared his throat. Now, if only he could find Kendra.

His fears returning, he asked, "Are you sure none of you have seen Kendra?"

"Not since she left for your place," Lupita said, turning to face Jack.

Alarm shot through him. "She should have been back by now. *Before* now."

Violet frowned. "I thought the two of you would be together."

"No," Jack said tersely. "I need to find her."

"Maybe she's just enjoying the ride."

"I don't think so," he muttered, ducking his head. He could confess his stupidity later. What mattered now was finding Kendra well and safe.

"She could be in the barn," Lupita suggested helpfully. "She loves to be out with the animals."

"Well, she'd call if she had trouble," Violet added. "I gave her Mom's cell phone, you know, just in case, like we discussed."

Relieved to know that, Jack pulled out his own phone and dialed his mother's number, only to announce a few moments later, "The call went to voice mail."

Violet winced. "I probably forgot to reset the ringer. We turned it off at the hospital, remember?"

"I'm going to check the barn," Jack said, striding for the door. "One of you go up and check her room. Call my cell if you find her."

"I'll go," Violet volunteered, rushing off in one direction as Jack went in another.

Nipper met him in the courtyard. Jack absently addressed the dog as he moved rapidly toward the fence. "You seen Kendra, boy? I need to find Kendra."

The dog capered ahead of him, heading straight for the barn, but whether because he understood Jack's question or surmised Jack's destination, only God knew. Breaking into a trot, Jack prayed it was the former.

Chapter Fifteen

The barn door stood open. Jack took that as a good sign and hurried inside.

"Kendra?"

She didn't answer, but even as he ran to check the stall, he saw that Mouse had been returned and tended. Thanking God, he sagged against the metal railing. At least she hadn't been thrown, adding physical injury to the pain he'd already dealt her. He still needed to see her, though, to talk to her.

"Kendra!" he called again, glancing around the cavernous building.

Failing to catch sight of her, he headed for the rear of the barn, thinking that she might be playing with the ducks. He hadn't walked four steps when Tom—Thomasina, rather—darted in front of him, a much slimmer version of her former self.

The kittens. Thomasina had obviously delivered the kittens.

Remembering that Kendra had prepared a box for

that very event, Jack turned around and made for the prep room. "Kendra. Talk to me!" Heart pounding, he told her, "I'm sorry about earlier."

But Kendra was not in the tack room to hear him. He got out his phone and dialed Violet's. She answered almost instantly. "Sorry, Jack, she's not here."

"Well, the horse is," he reported, puzzled. A horrible thought seized him.

She'd gone. Kendra had left him.

"Oh, God, no. Please," he prayed, ending the call. Distraught now, he began yelling, "Kendra! Where are you?"

Had she regained her memory? Had she called someone to come for her, someone from her past? He might never know, and against that possibility every other mystery in his life paled to insignificance. He staggered back, nearly felled by the idea of losing her.

"Kendra! Where are you?"

"Here," she mumbled, frowning at the words that did not fit the scene. The voice belonged to Jack, all right, but he knew where she was; he was right there with her, smiling and holding her hands in his. Except...she wasn't really there herself.

Kendra sat up, groggily pushing back her hair as the dream dissolved. She looked around, her breath catching, and realized where she was—and where Jack had to be. Scrambling over to the edge of the loft, she looked down and saw Jack standing just outside the prep room. She called out to him.

"Jack!"

His gaze zipped straight up to her. "Thank God!"

"What's wrong?" she began.

At the same time, Jack started forward, saying, "I'm so sorry. You were right. I was avoiding everyone and everything, but it won't happen again, I promise. Just don't leave."

Thrilled, Kendra started down the ladder. "How did you know I'd spoken to the sheriff?"

"You spoke to George?" Jack asked. "What did he say? No. Never mind. It doesn't matter. I don't want you to go. Not now, not when you regain your memory, not ever."

Laughing, she looked back over her shoulder as she stepped down—and missed the next rung entirely. Her weight shifted, sending the ladder rolling in one direction and her body in the other. Jack yelled for her to watch out, and then she hit the ground, hard, her head bouncing like a rubber ball. She saw lights flashing as pain exploded inside her skull, then blackness.

"Kendra!" Jack's voice came to her through the inky darkness. Hands reached out to her, arms lifted and cradled her close. "Honey, look at me. Wake up."

She fluttered her eyelids experimentally then clamped them closed again as a kaleidoscope of images rushed at her. Thousands, millions of bits of information flooded her mind, leaving her gasping.

Reeling from the sheer volume of information, she tried to sit up, to let Jack know that she was okay, but he clasped her to him, rocking with her. She realized suddenly what he couldn't possibly yet know. Elated, she threw her arms around him. He gusted a great sigh of relief and crushed her tightly.

"Thank You!" he exclaimed. "Thank You."

She smiled. Then she began to laugh, wincing as pain lanced through her head.

"Sweetheart?" Jack's hand cupped her face. "Honey, are you okay?"

She managed a nod, relieved that her brain seemed fixed to its moorings and not ricocheting around inside her head. The pain had already begun to fade.

"Say something," Jack pleaded. "Talk to me."

"I remember," she croaked. She remembered it all. Everything. Every blessed moment that had been lost to her these past weeks.

Jack gasped, loosening his hold on her. She looked up to find him staring down at her with a strange look on his face. She nodded to let him know that he had heard correctly. On his knees, he dropped his arms and sat back onto his heels.

"Kendra?"

"It's Keira," she corrected, struggling up onto her arms, her palms planted on the ground. "That's why Kendra sounded so familiar. My name is Keira Wolfe. Wolfe with an *e*."

Jack sat down hard, his legs sliding to one side. "What do you remember?" he asked carefully.

"I remember," she said, smiling slowly, "why I left Amarillo."

Pulling up one knee, Jack draped his arm over it and swiped his hand over his face. "Go on."

She gave him the most pertinent fact first. "I'd just broken up with my fiancé."

Jack stared at her for a moment then shifted around, folding his legs. "Broke up, you say?"

Keira copied his position, touching her knees to his. "Yes. H-he insisted on this huge society wedding that I didn't want."

A smile spread across Jack's face. "You didn't want a big wedding?"

"It would just be me and a few friends," she explained, "and him with all his family, customers and social network, not to mention his political allies."

Frowning, Jack parroted, "Political allies?"

"He has political ambitions," she explained. "They overshadow everything else in his life, even me. He'd started saying that my work is 'dirty' and 'unfeminine,' and he didn't want me 'mucking around filthy farms,' as he put it." She blinked, straightening her spine. "I'm a veterinarian."

"What?" Jack laughed. "Well, *that* explains a lot!"

Keira gasped. "Merry, my boss, must be going crazy. I'd just joined her small-animal practice in an effort to please my fiancé, so she's probably managing fine, but she's got to be wondering what happened to me."

"We'll call her," Jack promised, "but first tell me how you wound up in an unregistered car with that veil on your head."

"It was the wedding planner," Keira clarified. "My fiancé, Drew, called me down to the dealership. He's a new-car dealer. In fact, he owns several dealerships in two states. Anyway, he knew I was upset about limiting my practice to small animals, so he decided to give me the car as an engagement present. He brought it in from his dealership in New Mexico, on consignment or approval or whatever they call it."

"That's why there was no record of it in Texas," Jack said. "Okay, that explains the car, but what about the veil?"

"When I got to the dealership, the wedding planner was there with all her books and samples and what have you." Keira waved a hand. "Drew more or less ambushed me with her." Keira had refused to go to the bridal shop and talk to the wedding consultant there, so he had known how she felt about the whole idea. "Since my grandfather's death," she explained, "it's just been me and a few good friends, so I wanted a small, personal wedding, not a show with a big write-up in the paper and a bunch of politicians I don't even want to know."

"I'm with you there," Jack said, grinning.

"He wanted to invite the governor," she recalled, upset all over again. "Apparently, if you donate enough money, you can do that."

"So he's rich, this guy?"

Keira shrugged. "I suppose. To tell you the truth, I don't really know. He certainly wants people to think he's rich. The ring I threw at him before I jumped in the car and hauled out of there was so big and gaudy I only wore it when I knew he was coming over." She shook her head, wondering why she'd ever agreed to marry the man.

They had met at A & M University. She had been a sophomore and he a senior. After he'd graduated, they really hadn't spent that much time together, but he'd been so good to drive down when she had space for him, and over the years, it just became…normal.

"Things started to go wrong when I moved back to my grandfather's house in Amarillo," she said. She looked at Jack then and admitted, "I think I knew all along that I wasn't going to marry Drew, from the moment I accepted his ring."

One corner of Jack's mouth curled up, and he leaned forward until his forehead touched hers. "Good," he said. Just that.

It was enough to make Keira's heart sing.

He took her hands in his, asking, "So the veil…"

Keira reached up and touched the top of her head. "That silly woman stuck it on me, even after I told her—told them both—that I didn't want it!" She rolled her eyes. "The thing's worth a mint. It's some designer piece. I—I have to return it. And the car."

"We'll take care of it," Jack told her, squeezing her hand. "I'll have the car fixed and towed back to… Drew, is it?"

"Drew Knoel."

Jack frowned. "I know that guy. He's the one with his picture on the billboard above his dealership right there on Interstate 40."

Keira nodded, saying nothing about the supersize ego that had prompted the billboard. As far as she was concerned, Drew was the past—the distant past—and she had more important revelations in store for Jack.

Sobering, she said, "I know why I was going to Grasslands, Jack, a-and why I lost control of the car at that curve."

"It's okay," he murmured, shifting closer and slipping his arm around her. "It's okay. Whatever it is."

"My family," she whispered, her eyes filling with tears. "My parents and my older sister, they died in a crash at that very spot. I remember it was raining, and the tire blew as we were coming down the hill. The car hit a tree."

"They still talk about that wreck," Jack told her in a shocked voice. "Honey, I'm so sorry. I should've thought to check the records or—"

"You couldn't have known," she objected. "No one could have. I—I just wanted…my grandfather is buried next to them, out at the old Green Rest

Cemetery. He raised me, and when he passed about nineteen months ago, I brought him from Amarillo to lie beside my mother, his daughter." Her grandmother had died when Keira was just a baby, and her grandfather had buried her with her family down in Houston. Then he had moved up to Amarillo to be closer to his daughter, Keira's mom. "We'd agreed that when the time came, he'd be buried there with the rest of my family," she divulged with a sniff.

"Wolfe," Jack said, his brow furrowing. "Leon and…"

"Karen," Keira supplied in surprise. "Leon and Karen Wolfe, and my sister's name was Leila."

"I remember them," Jack breathed, "from church."

"That's why Mrs. Lindley thought she knew me!" Keira exclaimed. "My mom's hair was brown, but Grandpa always said I look just like her in the face."

"Your dad taught school."

She nodded. "History, and he coached baseball at the high school."

"I remember you, too," Jack went on excitedly. "You were just a little girl, and your mom used to put up your hair in two ponytails with these big bows, I mean *huge* bows."

Keira laughed through her tears. "I still have those bows in a box back at Grandpa's house in Amarillo."

"You know what this means, don't you?" Jack asked softly.

She shook her head, her heart racing.

"It means that this is where you truly belong," he whispered. "Grasslands is your home."

Grasslands. Not the ranch. Disappointment abruptly swamped her, but she somehow managed to keep her smile in place, murmuring, "It's something to think about."

"Think about this while you're at it," he told her, cupping her face in his big, capable hands.

He tilted her face up, and her heart did a double backflip as he slowly lowered his head. When his lips met hers, she moaned softly and closed her eyes, lifting her hands to his shoulders. Tilting his head, Jack pulled her to him, going up on his knees so that they knelt face-to-face. She slid her arms around his neck and put her whole heart into that kiss.

At first, just as last time, she was afraid to hope, to read anything meaningful into his kiss, but then she remembered how ardently she had prayed not to be separated from Jack. She had so feared that her past would keep them apart, but that was not the case. All that could separate them now was Jack himself.

Jack broke the kiss. He hugged her, tucking her head into the curve of his shoulder.

"I thought I'd lost you," he choked out. "I thought you'd left me."

"I meant to," she admitted. "It was bad enough when you were avoiding me, but when I realized how angry you were with me… I just couldn't stay here without being able to see you."

"I wasn't angry with you," Jack refuted urgently, leaning back so they were eye to eye. "I was just angry, period. Mostly, I was angry with myself for failing to find any answers for my family."

"That's not your fault. I pushed you into—"

He kissed her again, quite effectively shutting off the flow of words. Afterward, she could only sigh and lay her head on his broad shoulder.

"It was never about finding answers," he told her softly.

Surprised, she lifted her head, looking him in the eyes. "No?"

He slowly shook his head side to side. "No. It was about us. Don't you see? God used those trips and all of our problems to bring us together." He smiled, smoothing her hair with one hand. "It was no accident, my being out on the range that day just when you came along, your amnesia…none of it. Even as beautiful as you are, if God hadn't crashed your car right in front of me, I'd have walked away, and He knew that, so He literally threw you into my path and fixed it so I had to bring you home with me."

Hearing that, she threw caution to the wind and risked everything. "I love you, Jack."

Abruptly, he sank back onto his heels, his light brown eyes plumbing hers. "I think you mean that."

"I was in love with you even before my memories

returned," she confessed. "How could I not be? You took me in when I had nowhere to go."

"Wasn't no one else to do it," he drawled.

"You gave me a job."

He chuckled. "A job I didn't want to be doing myself."

"You trusted me with your deepest secrets," she tenderly pointed out.

"Turns out that a girl with no memories of her own is a pretty good listener," he quipped.

"And you made me feel safe when I was terrified."

"I always want to keep you safe," he said, sobering. Then he suddenly grinned. "And I won't even insist on a big wedding."

She blinked as the implications of that hit her. "Are you asking me to marry you?"

"I have to," he said. "You're the only one who won't let me get away with hiding from my problems. Besides, I can't move you into my house until you marry me."

"Jack!" She threw herself at him.

Laughing, he caught her and wrapped her in his arms. "I love you, too. I loved you before I even knew your name, before *you* knew your name. I loved you when I feared that you might belong to someone else. I loved the *idea* of you before you even showed up to give that idea a face, but I thought romance was out of the question for me, that everything else had to take precedence." He exhaled deeply. "I was a fool. There's nothing more important than what we have together."

"Oh, Jack."

"Everything else is still a mess," he warned. "All your questions are answered, but I still don't even know for sure who I am."

"Yes, you do," she insisted. "You don't know your true name because you don't know for sure who your father is. There's a difference in not knowing yourself and not knowing your name, believe me. I'm one of the few people in this world who can speak authoritatively on the subject."

"Okay," he conceded with a grin, "but wouldn't you like to know if you're going to be Mrs. Colby or Mrs. Wallace?" Lifting an eyebrow, he added drily, "Whatever happens, you won't be Mrs. Earl, I promise."

She laughed at that. And then she cried. She was going to marry Jack!

"I don't care. As long as you give me your name, I don't care what name it is."

"My name," Jack vowed, "and my heart."

Epilogue

They agreed, as Landon and Violet and Ty and Maddie had before them, that no wedding, however small, could take place until Belle awakened or Brian Wallace returned to furnish the family with some answers. Meanwhile, Keira would continue to live at the ranch and help Jack "feather the nest," as she put it, at *their* place.

Jack loved the notion of *their place.* Suddenly, the old rock house was no longer the Lindley place. Now it was *home,* even without Keira in residence, a place of peace and comfort, rather than simply a means to avoid the turmoil of his life.

"So I should change your address to the old, er, new house?" Pastor Jeb Miller asked, signaling to Sadie, the church secretary.

Jeb, Keira and Jack stood together on the grounds of the church in the waning daylight. Picnic tables arranged on the green looked all but ready to collapse beneath the weight of the many dishes arranged buffet style atop them, while blankets inhabited with diners created a crazy quilt pattern across the grass.

Jack chuckled. "To tell you the truth, Pastor, I don't even know what the address is out there. We can leave things as they are for a while."

"Ah."

Instead of signaling Sadie to stay where she was, the pastor folded his hands and rocked back on his heels. Jack traded a small, surprised smile with Keira. The kindly preacher seemed to be forming an attachment to the reticent secretary. Jack couldn't imagine why. Compared to Keira, Sadie Johnson was a colorless, almost invisible little soul, but he supposed that she probably suited the mild-mannered minister. Perhaps she triggered the man's protective instincts. Jack knew all about that, and he silently wished them well, provided, of course, that Sadie returned the good reverend's affections. She certainly appeared to, given the way her shy gaze flashed over Jeb's face and how tightly she clasped her hands together, unconsciously mimicking the pastor's stance.

"Yes?" Sadie said in a voice just above a whisper.

Jeb bent his head, giving her his full attention. "My mistake," he told her, "but since you're here, you can add your congratulations to mine."

Sadie looked around in confusion. "Oh?"

Keira lifted her hand, showing off the tasteful engagement ring that she'd picked out after she and

Jack had delivered the still-damaged car to Drew Knoel in Amarillo. After learning of Keira's amnesia, the brash auto dealer had insisted that he would take care of the matter. He had not, Jack had noted, tried to convince Keira to continue their engagement. Jack surmised that, as an aspiring politician, Knoel wanted to avoid any whisper of scandal, which seemed to be why he hadn't reported Keira or the car missing. Jack also figured that, being less idiot than fool, Knoel knew exactly who Keira would be marrying when that happy day arrived.

Keira's former boss, Merry, had been much more effusive in her relief and welcome when they'd stopped by the pet clinic. She regretted losing Keira's help and apologized for not questioning Knoel when he'd assured her that Keira had probably gone off to A & M to look for a position that better suited her. Given Keira's expertise in agricultural medicine, Merry could be excused for believing Knoel's story. Pleased when Keira had joked that she'd found the "perfect position," Jack had happily concurred that Merry should be kept informed about the wedding, as well as Keira's career plans.

They were still undecided if she would open her practice at the ranch or in Grasslands. Jack hoped to eventually build her a treatment center at their place and add an office onto the house for her. That way, everything would be at hand once the babies started coming. Their babies. The very idea made Jack's chest swell.

Sadie murmured appreciative remarks about Keira's ring and congratulated Jack on the engagement, color blooming in her face. Keira was trying to put the poor thing at ease when Johnson Parks bumped into her.

"Wow, Keira," the stumbling cowboy said, iced tea sloshing from the disposable cup in his hand. "Credit where it's due. You've really cleaned up our Jack. I hardly recognize him."

Smiling proudly, Keira turned to sweep a hand over Jack's shoulder. He'd donned his best jeans and brown felt hat with a clean, white shirt and a bolo tie with a silver concho for the occasion.

"I think he always looks great," she purred.

Jack smiled, hearing Parks jokingly ask, "Did you have to twist his arm to get him in that sport coat?"

"Sport coat?" Jack echoed, frowning at Parks's obvious shock as recognition widened his eyes. "What's wrong with you?" Jack queried, as the other man gaped at him.

Turning to point in the direction from which he'd come, Parks intoned, "If you're here, then who is that?"

Jack knew before he even turned. Grabbing Keira's hand, he jerked around, his gaze searching the scattered crowd until it came to the edge of the parking lot. There stood Grayson. It could be no other.

His twin wore his hair short and neat. The aforementioned sport coat, worn with a dark T-shirt and perfectly tailored slacks, lay snugly across his shoulders, one of which bore a sling that cradled his arm. In the other hand, he held a Bible. Jack knew, with dead certainty, that it contained a piece of paper bearing a handwritten note with the same wording as those received by him and his sisters. Correction. *Their* sisters.

"Oh, wow..." Keira breathed, starting forward with a laugh.

Jack quickly passed her, dragging her along in his wake as he felt himself drawn inexorably to his brother. He stopped short, staring at the man who stared at him.

"You must be Jack."

"You brought your Bible and note," Jack said, switching his gaze to his brother's hand.

"Yes. I brought them to show everyone, along with copies of Maddie's emails. I think we all need to sit down and talk about Dad."

"Brian," Jack corrected automatically.

Grayson said nothing to that. Jack stood there a moment longer, wishing he could shake his brother's hand. Then Keira slipped forward and gingerly hugged Grayson.

"I'm Keira, Jack's fiancée."

Gray's eyebrows rose at that, but he said simply, "Good to meet you. Both."

Jack smiled, partly because Keira was always leading the way in these things and partly because his twin brother stood right in front of him. Stepping up, Jack carefully embraced this man he hadn't even been sure he wanted to meet. To his relief and delight, Grayson folded his free arm across Jack's back, Bible and all.

Violet and Maddie ran up, breathless and excited. Jack stepped back just as Maddie threw herself at Grayson.

"Gray, you're here! I'm so happy to see you."

"There's two of you," Grayson teased, grinning at Violet. "Hello, other little sister."

Smiling, Violet wedged her way in to curl an arm about Gray's neck, just in the same way that she often did Jack's. Strangely, Jack was glad. He'd expected to be a little resentful, but instead he felt… right. That was his twin brother standing there. His *twin*.

"Now listen, everyone," Gray said, growing serious. "I have a plan to find out the truth. That's what we all want, right? The truth about the family."

A spurt of doubt shot through Jack. Their mother had been so determined to keep her secrets. Who knew what the truth might be? Wild possibilities flitted through his troubled mind, but then Keira slid her hand into his, and that one small touch grounded him.

Of course they had to find out the truth. They owed it to the family. And whatever came, they would face it together, as a family.

"Let's all go see Mom," he proposed, squeezing Keira's hand tightly. "Then let's take this brother of ours home. Show him what he's been missing."

Grayson shifted his weight. Jack understood what his twin must be feeling, but God would set it all right for him, for all of them. The look of love in the pretty hazel eyes of the woman at his side told him as nothing else could that the Lord God had a plan for each and every one of them.

* * * * *

Dear Reader,

Has your life ever been in such a mess that you didn't know how to pray? I think at some point we've all been uncertain what to ask for and what was best. Sometimes, we look at all the possible solutions to our problems and we don't see one that doesn't have unpalatable consequences. Fortunately, God's vision is better than ours, and He cares for us so much that when we don't know how to pray for ourselves, the Holy Spirit intercedes for us.

My dad used to say that the only true prayer for a Christian is "Thy will be done." He was right to teach that we should all submit ourselves to the perfect will of our Heavenly Father. We can take great comfort, however, in knowing that the Holy Spirit will intervene on our behalf, no matter how tricky the situation seems.

God bless,

Arlene James

Questions for Discussion

1. How important is it that we know about our pasts? Jack Colby thought it was very important until his curiosity resulted in his mother's riding accident. After Belle fell from her horse and wound up in a coma, Jack decided the past should be left alone. Was he right?

2. Have you ever found yourself prompted by an unconscious need to go somewhere or do something? After an ugly scene with her fiancé, Drew Knoel, Kendra found herself recklessly drawn to the site of a previous trauma. Does this seem reasonable to you?

3. Because Jack discovered Kendra after her auto accident, he felt responsible for her. Have you ever felt responsible for someone in a similar situation? If so, when, where and why?

4. Do you think it is possible that God chooses mates for us and brings them into our lives? (See *Genesis* 24.) Why or why not?

5. Twins are purported to have a special connection that other siblings do not share. Do you think this is true? If so, does the connection exist if they are separated at birth or before memories form? Explain.

6. Most people think that amnesia wipes away all memories, but that is not usually the case. Even when victims of amnesia forget their identities and entire pasts, they still recall how to walk and talk and perform functional tasks. Amnesia may not wipe out education or skills. Would you find amnesia frightening even if you could manage to do what you were trained to do? How would you react?

7. Kendra comes to a place where she doesn't even know if she wants to remember her past for fear that something from before will cost her the present. If you could choose to forget your past in order to maintain your present circumstances, would you? Why or why not?

8. Jack's guilt concerning his part in his mother's accident leads him to resist accepting his newly discovered siblings into his life. Because he pressed Belle for information she did not want to give, he felt discovering that information after she was unable to protest was unfair. Have you ever closed your heart to someone because of a tragedy? What happened?

9. Kendra's lack of memories left her without connections to anyone. This colored her perception of Jack's emotional rejection of his previously unknown sister, Maddie, twin brother, Gray-

son, and half or stepbrother, Carter. Was Kendra right to urge Jack to open his heart and fully embrace his whole family? Why or why not?

10. Jack's life is in turmoil. His mother is in a coma. Siblings he hadn't known existed suddenly pop up. His supposed father, Brian, is missing and possibly ill. He has a twin, a carbon copy of himself, for whom he has no affinity. Add to that a previous romantic disappointment and the sudden engagements of first one sister and then the other.... Wouldn't it be wise for a man in his position to avoid emotional entanglements? So why didn't he?

11. Kendra's life is also in turmoil. She has no memory of her past, no money, no place to live, not even a change of clothing. She doesn't even remember her real name! Wouldn't it be wise for a woman in her position to avoid emotional entanglements? So why didn't she?

12. Despite her lack of memories, Kendra seems to possess a type of emotional wisdom that Jack needs. From where might that wisdom have come?

13. Jack is a Christian, yet he is sometimes grumpy and obviously confused about what is best to do where his family is concerned. If you were

counseling Jack, to what Bible verses would you point him?

14. Kendra's memory returns after she bumps her head again, but her love for Jack remains even after she recalls her past. What if her memory had *not* returned? How would you have advised her if her amnesia had seemed permanent?

15. Jack and Kendra's story is pure fabrication. Their romance is based upon the supposition that God can and does arrange circumstances in our lives to bring us to the places and peoples He wills us to be and know. Does that ring true for you? Why or why not?